4<sup>th</sup> April.
18 Sept
7 Oct
30 June.
16 July

WO

Please return/renew this item by the last date shown

**worcestershire**
c o u n t y c o u n c i l
Libraries & Learning

70(

D0795479

# F.B.I. SHOWDOWN

At first, the two events seem uncon-
nected — except for their violent
nature. In North Carolina there is an
escape from Halifax jail. Whilst in the
southern state of Virginia, a vicious
mob lynches and burns a man alive.
But the Federal Bureau of Investigation is summoned when the escaped
convicts steal a car and cross the state
line into Virginia. More horrifying
murders occur, and F.B.I. operator
Leif Sorensen strives desperately to
untangle the twisting trail of escalating
deaths . . .

GORDON LANDSBOROUGH

# F.B.I.
# SHOWDOWN

*Complete and Unabridged*

## LINFORD
*Leicester*

First published in Great Britain

First Linford Edition
published 2010

British Library CIP Data

Landsborough, Gordon.
  F.B.I. showdown.- -(Linford mystery library)
  1. United States. Federal Bureau of
Investigation- -Fiction. 2. Fugitives from justice
- -Fiction. 3. Serial murder investigation- -
Virginia- -Fiction. 4. Detective and mystery
stories. 5. Large type books.
  I. Title II. Series
  823.9'14–dc22

  ISBN 978–1–44480–069–2

Published by
F. A. Thorpe (Publishing)
Anstey, Leicestershire

Set by Words & Graphics Ltd.
Anstey, Leicestershire
Printed and bound in Great Britain by
T. J. International Ltd., Padstow, Cornwall

This book is printed on acid-free paper

# 1

## Witness to murder

You can take your pick where you begin. Either in the prison farm at Halifax, North Carolina, with Egghead Schiller and Johnny Delcros and friends working around the State gas chamber (they don't electrocute murderers in the Old North State; they stick them in a room containing one easy chair and an unnecessary table, and release gas in on the sedative-filled candidate for Heaven, Hell, or wherever killers go).

Or we could start with little Hymie Kolfinkle, who took a picture of a man frying in oil.

Maybe we'll start with Hymie.

It's funny about men like Hymie, the newsreel cameraman. A man entirely undistinguished, and yet this fat little man triggered off a series of happenings that mushroomed to the size of the Bikini explosion and had nearly as great a repercussion on the American continent.

He didn't come much more than shoulder high on most men, little Hymie, and he had a big wife. In the first years after marriage she used to make life hell by threatening to go back to mom; and in these last many years she just wouldn't go back. He was a very depressed man.

That late May afternoon he was sitting high up on the Crombie Range, where the leaves on the trees still retained their green freshness, and the grass in the ditches was tall and succulent, unlike on the plains below, already going sear and yellow under this near-tropical sun.

He was looking into the descending sun through the orange visor on his stationary car, and he was wishing he had the guts to put an end to his life. He used to like to think of such a thing; in fact it was nearly the only thought that made him cheerful.

He liked to picture the shock it would give his wife when she saw him brought home and realised to what a state her nagging had reduced him. Yeah, and the neighbours would talk together indignantly and would maybe not speak to her for weeks, and that would surely burn her up.

After a while Hymie sighed and started the car. Sitting there did no good except make him late for reaching the town where he was to spend the night.

Hymie was Number Nine on the list of cameramen with the company. They had nine operators . . . He got the little jobs, like the coverage of a newly appointed smalltown mayor, or pictures of some new-born lambs to go with the Easter pictures, or one-and-a-half minutes of a woman speaker from Boston addressing the local Women's Guild. That sort of job particularly depressed him. Always those women speakers from Boston reminded him of the wife he was trying to run away from.

The other eight cameramen got sent on the choice assignments, to Florida in the winter season to show jaded northerners how the other half lived, to Sun Valley and other mountain resorts, and to all the big, exciting disasters, natural and man-made, that daily assault the American headlines.

'Me,' he thought, turning slowly down from the blessed coolness, 'me, I get the dirt.' And he felt very low and unhappy at the thought of it.

And yet little Hymie Kolfinkle got the biggest scoop of any cameraman, though he didn't realise it himself at the time.

He was about eight miles from that lusty, growing town of Warren Bridge when he ran into a fast-moving convoy of cars. He had come down the last of the gradients from the Crombie Range, and was about to pull into the main road to Warren Bridge when a big, expensive car, fronted by a chromium grin that screamed of dough in the owner's bank, flashed along towards him, braked hard and then turned towards the Crombie Hills. Following close behind came somewhere around twenty or thirty other cars, nearly all big and expensive-looking.

Hymie noticed that all were filled to the last seat and the occupants all seemed to be men. And clearly, the way they played follow-my-leader, they were all together in this expedition.

They were cutting the corner so fine, after the first few cars, that Hymie had to sit and wait, without being able to pull on to the main road. He felt so depressed he couldn't feel worse at being held up by the arrogant cornering of the convoy, and he just sat there and watched apathetically . . .

All the same, he received a curious impression from the occupants of the cars though he never heard a sound from any of the people in them.

He had a feeling of intense if suppressed excitement. Of emotion at fever-heat.

It was a similar sort of feeling you got at election time, and again when men left their wives and got together for some convention in a city where no one knew them.

Hymie tried to think of some convention that might be on at the moment around this part of Virginia, but failed. He didn't know this part of the country very well. He wondered what they were up to, and thought that maybe they were going to some place where there would be food and drink and someone to talk to. Hymie liked food and drink, but when he was depressed, as now, he liked even better to have someone to listen to his confidences about his wife.

It was on the impulse of the moment, then, that when the last car swooshed round the corner on tyres that skidded a little in the crunching gravel thrown up at the side of the road, Hymie suddenly pulled the wheel completely round and tailed on at the rear.

The sun was going down, but it was still hot and there was plenty of light. The party didn't go far. There was a wooded draw that came out on to the Crombie Hill-road just where the cultivated fields ended. It was a very lonely, desolate place. As they turned up the rutty dirt road that wound between the sparse, stunted oaks, Hymie thought it was a queer place for a lot of men to go for enjoyment. Then he thought maybe they were going pigeon-shooting and would then have a barbecue in the cool of the evening, and that seemed reasonable except for the fact that soon there wouldn't be light enough to see any pigeons.

Before he had time to think of another solution to the minor mystery, he realized that they were stopping. He also realised that they were in an open space that was like a cup amongst the little, tree-covered hillocks all around, and they were out of sight of the main Crombie Range road.

Some of the cars just stopped anywhere, but most of them pulled into a rough circle around a solitary oak that was rather to one side of the cup-like glade. Then everybody got out, and Hymie, for all his depression, was out as soon as anyone.

He went straight across to a group who were doing something to the baggage compartment at the rear of a big sedan. Hymie heard bottles clink together and said, 'Hell, but I got a thirst that makes blotting paper look like — ' He couldn't think what to make blotting paper look like, and anyway no one was listening that long.

Some bottles of cold beer were being handed round and Hymie got his hand there before anyone and was first to start drinking. For a depressed man he wasn't slow, little middle-aged Hymie.

They were all drinking when a big man came over. He had the fleshy body and ponderous limbs of a Hermann Goering, and he wore plenty of jewellery and a suit that was loud in an expensive way. He seemed to be a leader of this party, for everyone listened as he gave orders.

He growled, 'What'n hell, you should be watching the road, not drinking so soon. Keep a look out down the track, so that we're not surprised by any damned busy-bodies.'

One of the men — they all looked pretty prosperous, Hymie noticed, looked like well-to-do businessmen out on a spree — detached himself for a moment from the neck of his bottle. He made a smacking noise of appreciation and said, 'Hell, Frank, you don't expect anyone buttin' in here, do you?'

Frank's eyebrows came suddenly together as he glared back down the track. He growled, 'What are these cars, anyway? Find out before we start. For crissake, we can't have people we don't know looking on.'

The party turned, Hymie among them, only Hymie wasn't bothering to stop drinking while he looked. There were plenty more bottles of beer in that luggage compartment, he had noticed, and right now he could do with several himself.

Two cars were jumping up towards them. Frank was glaring down at them as though exasperated. He was saying, 'Why do people have to pick on this place tonight? You don't get a car in a fortnight normally, and tonight . . . '

Then another man, with a thin nasal, northern twang, interrupted. He said, 'Quit worrying, Frank, They're some of our cars. Heppy got a blowout, coming along Glades, an' a coupla other cars stopped to give him a hand. One came on after; guess these are the other two.'

Hymie did stop drinking then. He realised abruptly that strangers weren't wanted in this party, and he had blundered into it under circumstances that had momentarily misled these men.

But as he stared back down the track he was thinking that at any moment now they were going to discover him. They were expecting two cars — what would they say when three came?

Hymie decided to get around as much beer as he could before they started to look for a strange car in their midst, As he drank he saw the two cars come roaring up, and then saw a third back among the trees.

He waited for the exclamation that would prelude his exposure, but surprisingly none came. Then he realised that all the men, including Frank, were momentarily distracted by the bottles in the luggage compartment. The last car was within the circle by the time they straightened up and took another look round.

Frank held a bottle by the neck and spoke again before departing. He had the kind of red rough face that comes from playing golf a lot, and the chins and facial curves that come from talking golf in the clubhouse for long hours after . . . and drinking along with the talking. He said, 'Now look, you just keep watch back there like I said. Start blasting your horns if you see anything. Get me?'

They stopped drinking long enough to assure him they'd got him, and at that he swung his big limbs into motion and went across to the big automobile that had led the party. Hymie, watching along the top of an inverting bottle, saw him call and wave to some other sporting types like himself, and they all came across and pulled a big bundle out of the back of the car.

What followed took place less than thirty yards from where Hymie stood drinking, so that he heard and saw everything quite clearly.

So, when he noticed that the long bundle was a gagged and bound man, he jerked the bottle away from his lips and stared.

He saw them drag the prisoner upright, and there was an unnecessary roughness in the way they handled him. Again Hymie had that feeling of excitement

— an excitement that had a touch of mob-hysteria about it. And then he knew that these men were up to something big and bad and against the law, and he stopped drinking because he didn't like being mixed up in illegal activity. He had also begun to get an idea of what was going to follow, or he thought he had . . .

Frank was the centre of the group. He was doing a lot of shouting and working himself up into an anger. Hymie, who was small was in consequence an observer and not a doer of things, and he knew the signs because he had seen them many times before. Frank was wanting to do something that most men can't do in cold blood, so he was working himself into a fury in which he'd be able to do anything that his bullying, sadistic soul demanded.

Hymie looked around at the rest of the party and thought that there was probably not much to choose between any of them and Frank. Probably it was this common denominator of sadism that had brought them together in the first place.

They took the bonds off the prisoner,

except for the ones that tied his wrists together. Then they shoved him roughly from behind and made him walk across to the solitary oak in the glade. Hymie looked up and saw a right good lynching branch there, and the idea came to him that though the light wasn't the best right now, he'd maybe get some good pictures of what would follow.

He walked across to his car. He didn't sidle across, didn't make any furtive little movements that could have made men suspicious. The idea just came to him to get some pictures, so he stumbled across the open ground and got his smallest camera out and no one took any notice of him.

That was the incredible part of the whole business, how Hymie got his pictures with everyone there to see him taking them, and nobody getting het up or anything.

The truth, of course, was everybody assumed that Hymie must be all right to be there, and when he sat himself on top of his car nobody looked at him because of the absorbing tragedy that had begun under the oak tree away from the cameraman.

So he sat and from time to time took shots of the murder of a man by this blood-lusting mob.

Frank was doing most of the pushing and talking, but a few of his friends weren't much behind. One of them, a man not much bigger than Hymie, but without Hymie's fat weight, tore the tape off the man's mouth and then hit him on the side of his chin. Hymie saw something white fly out of the prisoner's mouth and guessed they were dentures.

The little man was shouting excitedly. 'Now talk, you son of a — ! Now let's hear what you got to say!'

But the man couldn't do any talking for the moment. He stood there in the last rays of sunshine, and the way his pursed up mouth moved around Hymie guessed he was tasting blood from the blow.

The prisoner had turned, so that now Hymie could see him clearly, and he got some excellent pictures of him standing there.

He was a pretty tall man, though a

stoop robbed him of height. He was very spare and middle-aged, and he didn't have much hair except just above his ears. The way he screwed up his eyes, Hymie thought that he probably wore glasses normally.

Without his teeth he looked to have a very small face, but most people do look like that without plates to lengthen their faces.

He stood and faced his aggressors, and his sunken features showed no trace of fear. Frank was working himself into a passion of rage.

'Goddamn him,' Hymie heard him shouting. 'Lynching's too good for the buzzard. So why don't we do what the Ku-Klux-Klan would have done to him? What say we burn him, eh?'

He was bawling his head off, getting himself excited and trying to work up the passion of the crowd at the same time. And they didn't need much stirring. They had come here for a lynching, so they were mostly much of a mind, and burning a man seemed a more interesting variation on the theme.

A lot of men started shouting along with Frank, and they all put a growling note into their voices so that it sounded very stark and jarring up in those foothills with the peace of evening closing in around them.

Hymie had an idea that a few of the men said something against burning the prisoner, but they didn't shout so loud as Frank and they shut up very soon, as if they weren't too minded what happened, anyway.

The little fellow who did a lot of sonofabitching came up with a rope and started to tie the prisoner to the oak. Then someone else started to collect dry sticks, but Frank roughly told him, 'Don't be a dope! We got better ideas than that,' and went away and then came back with a can of gasoline.

The prisoner was doing some talking now, as if realizing which way the mob was heading, but Frank kept shouting for him to shut his goddamned face, and that kept most of the crowd from hearing what the fellow was trying to say. Frank was red-faced and excited. This was the moment he had been leading up to, but he didn't show the pleasure that the scene gave him because that wasn't the part he was playing right then. Instead he had to keep up this fearful rage, this anger that seemed natural upon righteous indignation.

And somehow you don't enjoy things as much when you have to keep yourself red-eyed with fury all the time.

Everyone had been drinking heavily in those short minutes after reaching the glade, and it was showing effect. The voices of passion were thickened and slurred, and some of the movements uncertain.

But they got their prisoner tied to the tree, though he began to struggle as if now in panic. It was too late. The little fellow got so excited that he left off tying him and started to beat him about the head, but the rest of the men shouted him off because he kept falling in their way.

Hymie, his back to the last red rays of the sun, kept shooting the scene. No one was watching the back road now.

Frank stood back from the prisoner

and then whooshed the gasoline out of his can. It fell in a high arc over the prisoner and the tree trunk, and he kept swinging the can forward and sending further gasoline out over the man.

About the third throw the man started screaming and struggling frantically in his bonds. Hymie, his stomach tightening guessed that some of the gasoline had gone in his eyes and it was burning.

The screaming seemed to excite the men all the more, and Frank led them in a shouting match against the helpless prisoner.

'Scream, you buzzard — '

'Yeah, listen to yer damn' croakin' voice fer the last time — '

'The hell, you bin makin' a noise all your life, it's right you should go out makin' one now!'

They were more than half-drunk and they were baiting their enemy. The fact that he was completely helpless and incapable of protecting himself seemed only to bring out the devil in them. They were without pity at that moment, though many were to waken later and wonder what in hell had made them behave like that.

Then Frank struck a match and threw it forward. It seemed to go out for a second, and in that moment an eddy of night breeze wafted raw gasoline fumes across to where Hymie sat quietly atop the roof of his sedan, operating his camera.

Then there was a sudden, soft-roaring sound and a pillar of red fire leapt into the branches of the old oak tree.

Hymie didn't stop his camera now, didn't take it away from that writhing, burning figure that screamed away his last tormented moments on Earth.

And Frank and a few of the ringleaders were close to that pyre, and the red flames lit up their savage elated faces; and now they did not attempt to disguise the sadism which had actuated them and brought about this tragedy.

The screaming went on, high and awful. Someone shouted, 'There ain't enough gasoline, I reckon,' so Frank stood out for all to see and tossed the part-full can with an underhand throw so that it landed right at the burning man's feet.

The grass was burning for a square yard or so around, and now more gasoline gurgled out of the can and added to the flames and sent them flaming up around the limbs and body of the writhing, agonised prisoner. Almost immediately after that the screaming stopped and the man stood silent in his bonds and then sagged. And then the bonds burned through and he fell on his face in the burning grass,

Just at that moment the gasoline can blew up, and small gouts of flaming fuel came shooting all around the lynching party. They scattered in alarm, and then, realizing there was no danger, they stopped running and started to laugh loudly to show they hadn't been seriously scared. It sounded wrong and indecent with that corpse roasting.

Frank started to marshal the party after this; he drove them to their cars and told them to get moving back to town. It seemed they were going to leave the charred body just like that. Someone must have said something on the subject, for Frank immediately turned and with grim humour said, 'What the hell, you don't think the cops are gonna look far when they see who it is, do you? That is, if he can ever be identified. Old Mouthy's given 'em so much trouble I reckon they'd pin a medal on us if they knew what we'd done.'

Everyone who heard laughed again, and again it held that false, strident note — the note that creeps in when men are out of their depth but are hard at it, trying to kid themselves they're all right, that nothing's going to happen to touch them. But Hymie noticed that a lot were pretty quick to get into their cars and drive away. You might have thought that some were suddenly sobering . . .

Hymie pulled into the column but he didn't follow them down the Warren Bridge highway. Where it joined with the Washington road by the big, new hatchery he pulled left and headed north through the night. Another car pulled out after him, and it made Hymie sweat because he had just witnessed a murder and this was one of the accomplices driving hard behind. But in time this second car pulled into a farm road, and then Hymie went on through the night alone.

He had changed his mind about staying in Warren Bridge overnight; instead he would drive to Washington, where he lived, and put up at some hotel if the gosh-darned politicians and military hadn't taken all the beds. He wasn't expected home until the following day, and he wasn't going to be with his wife one minute earlier than she was expecting him . . .

He felt something coming up within him, and he stopped and got out of the car and was sick by the side of the road.

He thought, hell, thinking of his wife on top of what he had just seen was enough to make any man empty his stomach. He drove on and wondered what the boss would say when he came in with that film he'd just shot.

# 2

## Jailbreak

It was in the no-talking period. Johnny Delcros had been using his eyes and again he was speculating. He said, 'Get someone out there — a dame, say — she could shine a mirror up into that swine's face an' he wouldn't know where he was shootin'.'

His lips didn't move. They shuffled round the prison compound, grey, dejected, listless men. The 'swine' — the cop with the automatic rifle up top on the wall — shouted, 'Sew your lips down there. If I catch the guys that are talking, I'll roast 'em!'

The noise went on; no one appeared to be talking, but everyone carried on with their conversation. Exercise was a good time to exchange views on a variety of subjects, starting with the prison diet, going through discourses on the characteristics (generally unfavourable) of their warders, and even including speculation on the possibilities of — escape.

A number of men were committed to it. Johnny Delcros, with Egghead Schiller and a man named Joe Guestler were perhaps the ringleaders. There were about a dozen planning a break, all long-term men with only a part of their sentences completed. Delcros was in for another five years — he had been convicted on five charges of robbery with assault. One of the charges hadn't been his, and he lived now with a sense of grievance and injustice.

Schiller — he'd never had any hair since the day he was born, but had never quite realized what a handicap it was in his life of crime — Schiller was in on a ten-year rap and had served two only. Guestler was one of the Savannah Gang and he'd got life for his part in an automobile hold-up in which a girl had been assaulted and her escort killed while trying to stop them getting away. Erd Savannah had been given full penalty, and Guestler was lucky to have got away with life.

Louie Savannah, Erd's kid brother, Ed

Hankman, Jud Corbeta and one or two other boys were in on the proposed break. Hankman and Corbeta were both part of the old Savannah Gang and were serving fifteen years apiece. Louie, who had only been eighteen at the time of the stick-up, was also in for fifteen.

That length of time all in one place isn't to be contemplated calmly, so the Savannah Gang had got together to plan a break out. They weren't getting far when Egghead Schiller and Johnny Delcros were invited to join in the attempt. Egghead was Johnny's pal, and Johnny knew of a way of getting guns into prison. He wouldn't tell anyone, not even Egghead, how he did it, but they knew he wasn't talking tall words because one day he showed them a Smith & Wesson .38, and a week later he had ammunition for it. Egghead had an idea it was Johnny's girlfriend who brought the stuff in, and one of the warders was paid not to look when the things were passed. He couldn't see how else it could be done.

But Johnny had the damnedest ideas for a prison break. His idea was to get enough guns, start shooting and rush the wall, get over and drop down to where his dame would be waiting with a fast car. That was the only thing the Savannah Gang could think up, also.

Egghead used to listen, but didn't say anything. This day he heard Johnny come out with his theory about blinding the warder up on the wall with a reflecting mirror and then he told him what was on his mind.

They shuffled round, heads bent, dust coming up from the sun-dried concrete as their feet stirred it into motion. Egghead looked up at that high concrete wall, with the catwalk twelve feet above their heads, and the railed walk right on top of that twenty-foot high ring of ferro-concrete. There were guards leaning along that top rail, and more guards lounging about the catwalk.

Egghead looked everywhere but at Johnny Delcros, while words came thin and harsh through his tight-drawn lips. And he said, 'You got somep'n crawlin' in your head if you think I'm gonna try'n get over that wall with you.'

Johnny looked everywhere but at Egghead and snarled, 'Hey, you ain't got cold feet, have you?'

Egghead said, dispassionately, 'I would have, ef I joined in a break over the wall — permanent cold, I guess, along with the rest of me.' He looked at one solitary white cloud that drifted against the blue of the North Carolina sky and whispered, 'I got me better ideas, Johnny. But they don't include the Savannah mob.' He made a nasty sound in his throat. 'Them dumb clucks!'

That was better — Egghead wasn't quitting and was talking of other ideas.

Johnny said, quickly, 'If you got better ideas, Eggy, you don't go without me, see? I'm gonna bust outa this place, if it's the last thing I do.'

Egghead pacified him. 'Sure, Johnny, we bust out together when we go, but we don't need more'n you an' me, so we don't say anything to the Savannah outfit, see?'

They shuffled around on probably the last circuit before the whistle went for form up for the cellblocks. Egghead spoke

27

with care, stopping when any of the prisoners were near enough to hear. It wouldn't be nice for them if the Savannah mob got to know they were being double-crossed — even in jail things could happen.

Egghead's voice came thinly to the fight-calloused ears of his buddy. 'I never did like the idea of rushin' that wall. One or two of us might get over, but what ef you'n me stop this side o' the wall with a bullet in us? That'd be no go, now, wouldn't it, Johnny?

'So what? So I got to doin' some thinkin'. We'll let the Savannah boys go ahead with their plan, but we'll sneak out ahead of 'em, see?'

Johnny said, 'Why don't we tell 'em, Eggy? It would be better, in case they find out themselves. They're poison, that mob.'

'Sure they're poison. That's why we say nothin' — nothin', d'you hear, Johnny? You'n me'll make this break together. There'll be no room for the Savannah mob an' ef we tell 'em, d'you think they'll let us go without 'em?'

A prison guard came down and started shouting for fall in. Johnny said, viciously: 'I want for to paste him cross the mouth before I leave this joint. For why? Because that guy shoves us around more'n any other guard, an' I don't like being shoved around.'

Johnny wanted to hear the rest of the plan.

He got it over the evening meal. Egghead spoke above the noise of a thousand prisoners eating. There was a lot of noise, because the men said the food was getting worse and it had always been moderately lousy. Some of them set up a clamour with their plates and mugs, but it didn't get them anywhere and they shut up when the prison guards swooped quickly down among them. But it was a good opportunity for Egghead to get on with his plan.

'Remember the time they gave Erd Savannah the gas? They got a workin' party to clean up the death chamber the day before, remember? You'n me were on that job. We had to wash down the paint, scrub the floors and put a shine on everything. You'd have thought they were afraid Erd might take his custom to another jail ef he didn't like the look of his last sleepin' room.'

Johnny spoke through a mouthful of slush, cynically, bitterly. 'That wasn't for Erd. That was for the Governor, who's a sensitive li'l lily an' doesn't like to see dirt, the lousy sonofasoandso.'

Egghead got impatient and said, 'Sure, sure, I know all that. But — d'you remember the covers for the walls an' auditorium seats? The ones to keep the muck outa the gas holes? They got sent away for a quick clean, so's they could be put up again when the show was over.'

Johnny said, 'We took 'em to the laundry chute and dropped 'em down to the bin.'

Egghead said, 'We gotta fix ourselves on to that cleanin' up party next tine they fumigate anyone. Next time we're goin' down that chute together, see?' Johnny forgot and started to look at Egghead, recovered and stared down at his plate of food again. Egghead's voice went on, 'That bin's only a floor below. I guess it won't hurt us. And it opens into the loading bay where the laundry truck is!'

Johnny was rapidly cottoning on.

Egghead whispered, 'Don't you see, Johnny, that's better'n goin' over the wall with the Savannah mob. They'll be on the run from the second the break's attempted. Now, us, we might get half an hour or an hour's start before anyone sees we're missin'.' He leaned closer. Louie Savannah saw the action, and slowly put down his spoon.

Egghead said, 'We gotta have guns, both of us, that's all. We stick the truck driver up, then lie back among the baskets an' let him drive out through the gates. Ef he double-crosses us, we give it him in the back of the head.'

'An' when we get out of the district?' Johnny with the heavy, fight-marred countenance was better with his fists than with his brains.

'We still give it him in the back of the head,' Egghead growled. 'I ain't comin' back into this place, Johnny, no, not never. So I guess this time it don't matter what I do when I tote a gun.'

Johnny said, savagely, 'Bud, I'm right with you! This babe's another they won't bring back alive. Another five years in this place? Guess I'd be screwy as heck by that time, Eggy, just as you say, we go out together an' we don't ever come back, no, not never!'

When they were told to stand back of their benches and march off to the blocks, Louie Savannah got a whisper across the table. 'What's cooking, you guys? You doin' a lotta talkin' just now. Shoot the works?'

Johnny looked quickly at Egghead. It was only a fractional glance, but it told Louie they were up to something and were hiding it from him. Johnny came back across the table as they picked up the mark-time with their ill-fitting prison boots. 'Aw, gee, Louie, it ain't nothin'. Just a ball game we'd like to see in Charleston.'

Louie said, 'Yeah?' and then again, softly, 'Yeah?' and then turned to look for Joe Guestler. He was arrogant, young Louie, and no sort of man. Now that Erd was gone he thought he should be boss of the outfit, and he tried to say what should be done in their planning. But he wasn't like his brother when it came to organising, and that was why they hadn't got anywhere with the breakout to date.

Egghead saw the look and said. 'He's on to us, damn it. Fer crissake play the dummy or we'll be in jake with the Savannah boys!'

They made their break seven weeks later. Seven weeks isn't a long time, but seven weeks in jail can seem an eternity, and after a time Johnny got tired of waiting and wanted to try for a break over the wall, just as the Savannah boys were urging.

But Egghead said no, a wall break was no dice, and he talked Johnny out of it. Acting on Egghead's instructions, when the Savannah mob got impatient and wanted to start things, Johnny told them he hadn't got enough guns in for them yet. But to keep them quiet, he got in three guns and then some ammunition for the Savannah boys, with the promise of another couple to follow. He and Egghead already had flat .38 automatics . . .

A man was gassed in the lethal

chamber after three weeks of waiting — he had croaked a young girl who wouldn't play the game as he wanted her to — but neither Egghead nor Johnny Delcros got on the working party to clean up the place.

They were more fortunate when it was Parry Galowen's turn to take the last walk. Parry was a man thoroughly respectable at heart. He believed in the institution of marriage, and in fact had had several wives. The trouble was, they had insisted on remaining well and healthy when it would have suited the elegant Parry to have been a widower. So, Parry eased them into a happier world.

Now Egghead Schiller and Johnny Delcros were helping to ease Parry out of the world, and by all accounts Parry wasn't liking the idea.

As they shuffled off to get some cleaning materials, Johnny said, 'I just bin talkin' with old Rocky.'

Egghead kept his mouth shut and said, 'What about old Rocky?' shuffling along. Rocky — Philip Whitwam, nicknamed Rockefeller because he was forever babbling about the millions that had passed through his hands — was Johnny's cellmate.

'Rocky's got on to the breakout.'

Egghead jerked round quickly, surprised. 'Ours — on the laundry truck?'

'Naw!' Johnny drew his share of the cleaning rags and tramped out of the room and along the corridor to the lethal chamber. When it was safe he continued, 'He's heard about the Savannah boys' plan. He thinks we're goin' out with them. So he wants us to do something when we get out.'

'Yeah?' They were marking time in the corridor outside the chamber while an officer came up with the keys.

'He's mad at his brother. Old Rocky says he took the rap because there wasn't no sense in his brother comin' with him. But he says his brother ain't makin' no attempt to spring him from jail, like it was arranged. So he's mad at him, an' he wants us to look up his brother and beat him around the head a bit until he starts to do something.'

Egghead said, 'Like hell we'll beat

anyone around the head unless there's dough in it for us!'

Johnny Delcros got in a final whisper before the guard came along. 'Old Rocky says he an' his brother have got a million greenberries stashed away!'

Egghead was saying, 'Hell, he always talks in nice round figures,' when the guard was among them, bellowing to them to keep silent. They stopped marking time. In the distance a thin high wailing floated up to them from Death Row.

The guard grinned a big grin and said, 'Jeeze, the fuss dat guy kicks up. You wouldn't think we wus preparing his suite for him, would ya?' Some of the working party gave back the big laugh he was expecting, and that put him in good spirits.

They went in, and the screams of a man who had less than a day to live were lost as the soundproof door closed behind them.

There were really two rooms inside that soundproof door. One was a big room with a long glass observation panel all along one wall. Here the prison doctor, the Governor, various officials of the State and even a few Pressmen sat and watched while the prisoner took the last step out of this world. That room had to be prepared, too.

On the other side of the observation panel was a room not much bigger than a closet. One wall was perforated with pipe-inlets, which led to a battery of carbon monoxide cylinders outside. There was one easy chair in the room, with wooden armrests to which the prisoner would be strapped when they brought him in. There was also a small but very heavy table screwed to the floor.

No one knew why there was a table inside the gas chamber, but it appeared to be there out of custom, a relic of the days when a man was supposed to write his last letters before being taken out and hanged. Possibly the table was retained so that the solitary death chair wouldn't look quite so alone and sinister and so disturbing to the incoming candidate for death.

But Johnny and Egghead weren't

interested in the fittings. They had been here before — many times. On average that gas chamber was used every four or five weeks; for murder was a hobby to some and a profession to many more in North Carolina.

They were taut, now that the moment had arrived. Inside their prison shirts were their guns. They were watching all the time, waiting for the opportunity to get out to the laundry chute.

Then they realized that Joe Guestler, who was in the party, was watching them closely, and they guessed that they must be giving the show away somehow. Egghead was gathering the wall and furniture covers together. He whispered, 'Let's go now. This is our chance. Ef Joe Guestler follows, throw him down the chute, but he ain't goin' with us so knock him on the head first, see?'

They went past the guard and started the trek down the corridor to the chute. This was the big moment. Their mouths were dry, and a cold sweat had broken out over their bodies as they walked the long corridor that would seem so short to

Parry Galowen the following morning.

After they had shuffled a distance, they heard footsteps behind. Out of the corner of his eye Egghead looked at Johnny Neither turned; their faces might have given the show away.

They went round the corner at the end of the corridor. The chute was right in front of them, Egghead lifted the hatch and shoved his covers through, then Johnny did the same. Then they turned to walk back.

A man came round the corner. It was Joe Guestler. He started to say, toughly, suspiciously: 'You guys are up to somep'n! Louie says for to tell you it ain't healthy for guys to do things on their own. If you're plannin' a double-cross — '

Johnny hit him across the chin. Then Egghead brought the flat of his hand down on the staggering Joe Guestler's head, only in the palm was his automatic. Blood flooded down into Joe's eyes, but he didn't know it because he was unconscious as he was falling.

Working with frantic haste they hoisted Joe into the chute and let him ride down,

Then Johnny wiped up a few spots of blood that looked conspicuous on the polished floor and then clambered feet first into the chute and followed their victim. He came down slowly, but all the same his weight, landing on the unconscious Joe, couldn't have done him any good. Egghead gave Johnny half a minute to get clear, then slid down himself.

They were in complete darkness, standing on a yielding floor of dirty clothing for the laundry. Both started to push with their hands against the walls of the bin, guns ready for action.

Johnny suddenly whispered, 'Here!' and a crack of light showed. Egghead stumbled across. They pushed a little harder, and a door suddenly gave and they looked into the brightness of a whitewashed loading bay.

At once someone shouted, 'What're you doin' there?' and immediately Johnny and Egghead came plunging out, guns raised.

A couple of uniformed guards were directing the loading of some laundry baskets into the back of the big, cream-painted prison truck. Hefting the baskets were a couple of prisoners. Ironically, one was old Rocky, Johnny's cellmate.

Egghead's voice crackled, 'Don't make a wrong move, none of yer!'

Four pairs of hands shot up immediately. As Johnny came backing round to where the prisoners were, Old Rocky whispered, 'I didn't know this was the way you planned it. Good for you, Johnny! Don't forget to see that brother o' mine!'

Johnny snapped, 'Into that bin,' and shoved the two prisoners into the closet where Joe Guestler lay bleeding among the cloths. The bolt outside wasn't very strong, but Johnny knew the prisoners wouldn't start to attract attention for a long time, so as to give them a chance to get away.

When he turned, Egghead was prodding the two guards into the cab of the truck, Johnny heard him say, thinly, 'You want to live longer'n Parry Galowen? Then you do as you're told, see? Drive out through the gates as if nothing's happened. We'll be behind among the baskets, and I'll be watchin' your face in the drivin' mirror, an' if I see you so much as bat an eyelid, so help me, I'll give you every round in this gat!'

The two men looked at each other. Then one said, very earnestly, 'Brother, if I so much as cough I'll know I deserve what's coming. You betcha we're gonna be good boys!'

Johnny covered them while Egghead got in behind the cab, then Egghead covered them while Johnny climbed in among the baskets. The engine started. They didn't move.

After a minute Egghead snarled, 'What in Hades are you waitin' for?'

The driver very carefully explained, 'What're we gonna do about them doors? Someone's gotta open 'em and shut 'em behind us.'

Egghead snarled to the man next the driver, 'Brother, that's your job. You do it — and remember we're coverin' you all the time!'

The guard got down, opened the big doors and they drove slowly out into the prison compound. Johnny covered him from the back while he slowly, reluctantly closed the doors on the loading bay. Then, even more slowly, much more reluctantly, he came and took his place next to the driver. He didn't look healthy; perhaps he was thinking of what could be coming to them.

The driver appeared a calmer, less imaginative man. Obligingly he started across to the big gates, with the armed guards above and all around. Crouching behind the baskets, muscles tautened ready to spring into action, they heard someone call, 'Okay?'

The driver said, 'Okay,' and then the truck lurched into motion again. Egghead at once moved forward so that he could see through the windscreen, while Johnny crabbed along the top of the baskets and watched the receding prison gates.

Egghead called, 'Nothin' wrong, Johnny?'

Johnny said, 'Nothin' wrong.' He came back, almost purring. He said, 'Eggy, that sure was a swell idea of yours! The way them guards is just standin' around, we'll be outa the state afore they wise to what's happened.'

Egghead said, 'Not in this truck. We gotta get a car that can fly.'

He was looking at the backs of the guards up front, wondering what to do.

Ten miles out on the Petersburg highway he gave the order to pull up. Then he made the guards get out. Now even the phlegmatic driver was looking uneasy. His mate started to say, 'We did what you said, so you boys needn't think of gettin' rough. We're still cooperative — mighty cooperative!'

He was looking at those guns. The driver looked at them and said, 'Yeah, an' we'll still do as you say.'

Egghead, green-eyed and mean, snarled, 'I don't like them clothes you're wearin'. I've a mind to make two vacancies on the prison staff.'

Johnny said, 'Aw, Eggy, let's just stuff 'em in a basket. It gets everyone peeved if you kill a warder.'

The driver's mate said, 'Brother, you don't know how I welcome those words.'

Johnny went and hoisted a couple of baskets out on to the side of the road. They made the guards climb in, and then strapped them down and shoved them out of sight into a ditch. That was better than tying them, and much safer.

Egghead rubbed dirt all over his baldness, so as to make it less conspicuous. They drove another mile, then hid the truck among some trees. The longer it took the police to find the truck, the longer they would be in getting on their trail.

They walked the few hundred yards through a cornfield and then an orchard, and then came out on a rutty back road.

Johnny said, 'Now, that's luck,' because there was a smart coupé sitting beside the road waiting for them. They stood in the shade of the fruit trees and looked around for the owner. After a while Johnny spotted a movement up the hillside.

He grinned. 'The guy's up there, neckin'. He won't be thinkin' much about his car, I reckon.'

Egghead didn't smile. He never did have any humour. Johnny said, 'Give me a minute — I'll take care of this.'

A few minutes later, Egghead eased the car into gear and they went slowly down the lane.

Johnny said, 'Where to?'

Behind them, in the grass on the hillside, the owner of the car lay sprawled on the ground, bereft of his ignition keys and consciousness. A crying girl knelt alongside him, dabbing at the blood on his bruised temple where the butt of Johnny's automatic had struck him.

Egghead said, 'The heat'll be on any time now. Reckon we'll be safer over the Virginia border.' He pulled out on to the Petersburg road, and gave the coupé its head. They sat low in the car, so as to keep their prison clothes out of sight.

Hours later they were passing the sign that showed the state borderline. They were in Virginia.

They felt safe for the moment.

*They didn't know it was the biggest mistake they had made in their escape, taking that car into Virginia.*

# 3

## Problem film

Hymie came into the office next morning feeling unusually depressed. He had lost sleep during the night and felt grey and jaded, and the excitement of yesterday hadn't done his temperamental stomach any good.

He had also used up most of his footage, and the boss was tight on such things. Maybe the boss would bawl him out for using so much film on one subject.

So Hymie didn't say anything, and when the film was processed the boss and the two editors went into the projection room thinking they were going to see the usual routine stuff that fell to Hymie's camera.

The boss was giving orders and being critical as usual, until suddenly he saw men carrying a bound figure. After that he shut his fat mouth and saw right to the end of the film in silence.

Then he went out and crossed to his office, and Hymie and the editors trailed after him. Hymie let his plump body settle inside a big, leather-upholstered chair and felt for a cigarette. He found he had run out and he didn't like to ask for one, so he sat and felt even more fed up.

The boss, fat white hands playing with an expensive, gold-mounted presentation pen, said, 'What'n Hades are we gonna do with that film, Kolfinkle?'

Hymie said, weakly, 'I thought it was a good story.'

The boss's eyes looked worried inside his fat face. He complained, 'The hell, it's too good. Why should this happen to me?'

One of his editors spoke. It was G. Rudolph Reimer. Reimer was thin-faced, bitter, sarcastic. He was efficient, but that didn't make anyone except the boss like him.

He said, 'That film should be handed over to the police.'

The boss said, shortly, 'You're crazy. This company can't afford to get mixed up in things like that.'

Reimer said, thinly, 'It wouldn't be because you knew someone in that lynching party, would it?'

The boss kept his eyes down and Hymie saw that he was uneasy. He tried to sound surprised, but it kidded no one.

'I don't get you? Who should I know?'

Reimer said, evenly, 'Frank Descoign.'

It startled Hymie. He'd never met Frank Descoign, but he knew the name. The Descoigns ran a big chain of movie-houses all down as far as Atlanta in Georgia, and were about the biggest renters of their newsreels. Now he looked at the boss and began to understand.

The boss suddenly said, very hard in his manner, 'I never saw anyone I recognised. Bring that film up to me and we'll leave it in this office until I know what to do about it.'

Reimer's thin, cynical voice said, 'I wouldn't be surprised if somehow it got lost or destroyed if it came into this room.'

The boss snarled something, then pulled himself together and sent them off for the film. He walked over to the window when he and Hymie were alone together. After a while he said, 'You don't need to have to tell anyone what you saw, do you, Kolfinkle?'

Hymie hadn't even considered telling anyone, so he said, 'Why, sure, no, boss.'

So the boss turned and said, 'Maybe I can fix you a raise or something if you keep your mouth shut. God, I gotta do something. D'you think the Descoigns would buy our films if we handed this reel over to the police? And what'n hell would we do for money if the Descoigns pulled out on us?' He started to get worked up, and then Reimer and the assistant came in with the can.

The boss said, 'You can go, Kolfinkle. I want to talk to Reimer.'

Kolfinkle eased his fat torso out of the chair and walked across to the door. He knew he was being sent out of the office so that the boss could square Reimer and his assistant to keep their mouths shut. He thought that Reimer would probably be difficult. There was something hard and brittle about the fellar . . .

When Hymie had gone, the boss eased back in his chair and got a box of cigars out of a lower drawer. They were pretty good cigars at that. He shoved the box under Rudolf Reimer's nose and said, thick-throated, 'Help yourself. They're okay, these.'

Reimer watched him closely, his face thin and mottled red where the capillaries came near to the surface; there was a hooded effect to the droop of his eyelids that shaded cynical, sarcastic eyes. His head shook as he said, thinly, 'I don't go for cigars.' He went on, 'I don't hold with smoking at all,' and his voice was contemptuous and a rebuke at the same time, saying without words, 'Smoking's for small boys who never grow up.'

The boss's eyes flickered but he said nothing. He shoved the box before the assistant-editor, a plump young man named Rod Blackhurst. Blackhurst was too young for the job and didn't learn fast, but the boss wouldn't pay more, so Reimer had to manage with him.

Blackhurst hesitated before taking the cigar. He couldn't make this out; usually the boss gave rockets not cigars. So he watched the boss while his plump fingers fumbled with the cigar band.

The boss selected one, pulled out a pansy cigar-cutter at the end of a close-linked chain, then got his wet lips to work on the end until it was comfortable. And then he lit up. When he had finished he said, 'That film.' They all looked at the can on the table. 'It's hot. It'd cost me a fortune if it was shown. I can't afford the loss of business and the time hanging around the courts, see? So . . . you gotta forget you ever saw it, understand?'

Reimer said nothing but looked pink and mean and malignant. Blackhurst started to nod, started to say, 'Sure, boss, I get you,' and then tailed off because he didn't quite understand what it was all about. He fiddled around with the unlit cigar and cleared his throat noisily.

The boss looked at Reimer, then turned his fat-faced unpleasantness on to the uncertain Blackhurst. 'I guess you like your job here with me, Blackie?' Blackhurst nodded and cleared his throat again but said nothing. The boss went on, 'You wouldn't get another job like it, at your age. Okay, you keep the job as long as you keep your mouth shut about this.'

Blackhurst nodded dumbly. He didn't want to lose this job, because he was sure he'd never be able to persuade any other firm to take him on in a similar position.

The boss said, trying to infuse a note of kindness into his voice, 'You c'n go now, Blackie. But just remember . . . '

When they were alone together, the boss's manner changed. His voice came harshly now, and his eyes looked wicked within the deep folds of fat on his cheeks. He knew that Reimer wasn't to be moved by threats of dismissal, and he adopted other tactics.

He rapped, 'I know you, Reimer, know you better than you think.' Reimer glowered sarcastically, unmoved by the statement, apparently. So the boss went on, 'You're a born troublemaker, an' this seems something good to start a shindig with.' He pulped the end of his cigar with stumpy teeth, then delivered his broadside. 'If you think you are goin' to make trouble for me, just get it inside your head that I'd make a heck of a lot more trouble for you, brother!'

Reimer said, coldly, 'You tell me how.'

The boss said, 'I know somep'n about you, Reimer. You never served your time in the Army. You served three years in a Federal Penitentiary, didn't you?'

Reimer got to his feet. He said, 'So?'

The boss said, 'Right now they're purging the film world of all anti-American influences. Do dirt on me an' I'll blacklist you and no one'll ever take you on. That means you'll be washed out as a film editor.'

Now Reimer said nothing. Instead he crossed slowly to the door, his head bent as though brooding on something.

As he was going out, the boss threw after him, 'And you know somep'n, Reimer? I got other things here I know about you — not nice things.' He was tapping his forehead with a fleshy forefinger; there was a fat sneer on his heavy face. Reimer thought he might be bluffing, but he couldn't be sure. He said nothing and went out, closing the door softly behind him.

He went out on to the street, crossed to a bar and got a tall glass of light beer. He was thinking, all the time he was drinking. When only froth clung to the inside of the glass, he rose, a decision made, and crossed to a phone box. From a diary he selected a number and asked for long distance. When someone answered he spoke.

He spoke in German.

Back in the office the boss slipped on a light summer coat picked up the can and went for his car. He drove steadily out to his house in the country — an unusual performance for the boss, who lived around his desk most waking hours. His wife was surprised to see him, and was even more surprised when all he did was set fire to a can of film down at the bottom of their garden, then return to his office.

The boss should have felt relieved, now that the can of hot film was destroyed, but instead only forebodings of trouble assailed him. Intuitively he knew that there was going to be trouble over that film — plenty trouble for all concerned.

He decided that at the first opportunity he would fire Hymie Kolfinkle. Anyway, he couldn't afford to keep the guy, now he'd given him a rise.

# 4

## Enter the Feds

There was a police car standing by the cream coupé, a couple of cops with their hats off in the afternoon heat lounging in the cool shade of a tall tree by the curving, pleasant roadside. It was a lonely spot, without buildings of any sort in sight, though everywhere around were trees and cultivated fields that looked good farmland. The soil was the dark rich soil of Virginia, and the vegetation was lush, thick and green.

A big black sedan came fast round the bend, then slowed with a squealing of brakes and slipping tyre treads at sight of the police. The cops stirred and came slowly, questioningly, out on to the lane. Two men got out of the sedan. They were young, alert, pleasant-faced; they walked with the ease of athletes in constant, arduous training, and both were big enough to look down on most men.

The dark-haired, keen-eyed driver said, casually, 'Hyar, sergeant.' Then showed identification.

The sergeant, a jaundiced man who looked as though he played poker too long at nights, bit into a yawn and growled, 'Feds, huh? We bin expecting you. You took some time coming.'

The dark-haired G-man nodded. 'We got on to the wrong road. This side-track took some picking up — it isn't used much.'

The sergeant wasn't too pleasant. He said, with an abrupt laugh, 'If you Feds can't find a road — you can't find the fellar that pinched the wagon!' The heat had got at him, he had been suffering during the long wait by the roadside. 'Why'n hell we weren't told just to take this car back to the station, I don't know.' But he did know. He was just being bitchy.

The black-haired Fed ignored the unpleasantness and said instead, 'This is a stolen car with a North Carolina licence plate. You know that the moment a stolen

58

car gets run across a stateline it becomes an F.B.I. job.'

The sergeant felt foolish and hung around trying to think of something else to bellyache about. His companion, a patrolman, wasn't interested in anything at all right then, and just waited patiently to be told to get out of the stifling heat.

The G-men were looking into the coupé now. The dark-haired G-man asked, 'This been fingerprinted, sergeant?' The sergeant gave a surly nod, and wiped again at the gathering sweat on his brow.

He still felt mean and disgruntled, and he said, 'There are over two hundred thousand cars stolen in the United States every year. What's the chances on finding the fellars that took this jalopy, huh?'

There was a glint of humour in the big G-man's eyes as he turned, but he tried to keep it hidden.

He said, casually, 'We know who borrowed this one, sergeant.'

The sergeant paused in the act of putting on his cap. He repeated, 'You bin here three minutes an' you know who took this car out of America's a hundred and fifty million people? And we bin standin' there for two hours an' we ain't had a thought?'

The G-man wiped the moisture off his hands. He said, still twinkling, 'Two gentlemen named Schiller and Delcros rode in this car, sergeant. That's my hunch, anyway, and I'm willing to back it.'

The sergeant looked into the coupé to sec if he had missed anything. There seemed nothing to see, so he said weakly, 'You tell me, Ellery Queen.'

He was a good-humoured fellow, the big, dark G-man, and the bony, awkward G-man who was his companion seemed no less behind him in good nature.

'Pavlova and I were told that a couple of prisoners had escaped from the jail at Halifax, North Carolina, this morning. This car was reported stolen about ten or twelve miles from the prison. That's something to start on, huh?'

Now he pointed to the brake pedal in the coupé. 'See those scratches? And on the clutch and accelerator? Boots with nails in the soles did that, and they're not likely to have been caused by the owner of this bus because drivers of sleek coupés don't generally wear nail-studded footwear. In fact, not many people do, nowadays — but convicts wear 'em, don't forget.'

The sergeant wanted to argue, though he was already impressed. 'The hell, though, in this district we get a dozen cars pinched every day. Convicts don't pinch 'em all. And, look, around this farming district you'll find a lot of fellars that wear nail-studded boots. How d'yo know this coupé wasn't picked up by some farm clod back in North Carolina?'

The G-man said, cheerfully, 'I don't. You might be right, sergeant. But I'll still bet on my hunch. You see, I've noticed something, over the past few years. Like to know what it is, sergeant?'

The sergeant nodded dourly.

The G-man said, 'It's a funny thing, but almost every man we pick up for stealing a car wears slick, pointed shoes. They look dainty, but they hurt like hell if you have to walk in 'em. So what?

Suppose you don't own a car but you own narrow, pinching shoes that give hell to your dogs. And all around you are cars, all nicely unattended. After a time you get to arguing, 'What the hell, no one'll ever know,' and you get into a car and drive off. That's behind most of America's car thefts — the temptation to borrow a jalopy to save a walk.'

The G-man called Pavlova came in then. He had a voice like a rusty gate that suited his straw hair and freckle-mottled face. He came in with, 'Yeah, that's right, sergeant. We find that men with big comfortable boots like your farm-workers don't seem to need to borrow cars, but town boys with ritzy pointed shoes do it all the time.'

'So that makes it conclusive that the boys you want are a couple of escapees, huh? *But how d'you know the two are together?*' The sergeant was still trying to upset the G-men's theory.

The dark-haired G-man pointed across from the driver's position. 'The pile's scratched up on the carpet where someone else wearing heavy nailed boots shuffled around. Okay, that looks like two men snatched this car, and two men escaped from the prison farm. It's still not conclusive but when we compare finger-prints from this coupé, I'll bet they tally with the convicts'. If there are any finger-prints that is, convicts are wise guys.'

The patrolman opened up his mouth to speak now. The others had turned to watch a flivver come shaking down the lane towards them.

The patrolman said, 'You got it wrong, Fed. We got a general broadcast half an hour ago about the break-out, there weren't two prisoners got out — there were four.'

The G-men stared. The dark-haired one said, 'We heard two. They got away in a laundry truck. Maybe you got later information than we did?'

And the sergeant said, 'I never heard,' looking at the patrolman meanly.

'Sure,' said that man laconically. 'Sure you never heard. For why? You were sleepin', I guess, back there by the tree.'

The flivver came up, hesitated uncer-tainly, then stopped. The driver was dried lean by constant exposure to the hot Virginian sun. He was an old man, wearing jeans and a faded canvas jacket on top of a patched old shirt.

He said, in a voice that crackled like dry twigs breaking, 'I was just goin' for a cop. I guess there's need of one right bad.'

He looked uncertainly at the bulky G-men. The sergeant said, 'There ain't nobody bin pinching your car, has there, old-timer?'

The old-timer spat tobacco juice and looked surprised.

'Why, no, it ain't on account o' that,' he crackled. 'Nobody ain't bin pinching my old car, I guess; nobody ain't likely to. But I just went up to see Cal Turner 'bout the borry of a lead horse, an' when I got there I could see there'd bin trouble, an' . . . '

He ruminated for suitable words, and the sergeant got impatient. 'Well? Go on, get it out.'

'Well, I guess I found Cal with his head smashed in, an' just back of him was his wife an' she was dead an' I guess someone hadn't bin nice to her afore she died.'

The dark-haired G-man snapped into action. He wheeled on his companion. 'Get the car started!' Then he said to the old man, 'I'm Lief Sorensen, an F.B.I. operator down from our local field office about this stolen car here. My guess is that the thieves might be responsible for the crime you talk about, so I'm going up to see. You get down from your old can and come with us in our auto. And tell us your name.'

He stood close up, watching the old man as he descended. His eyes took in the clothing for stains that might have been blood, but he didn't see any. And there wasn't any scratches or bruise marks on that scrawny old neck and face.

The man said, 'Me, I'm Joe Finney.' He was out of the car when he said that, and seemed surprised when he turned to find the big G-man right there waiting with his hand out. He didn't see any reason for hand-shaking at the moment, but found he had to take Sorensen's big fist.

Sorensen said, 'I'm right glad to meet

you, Joe,' but he didn't smile and he didn't pump the hand up and down in hearty Virginian fashion. Instead he looked at it and stared especially at the nails. It was all done so easily and so quickly that the old man didn't notice anything. But the sergeant did. He saw it all. And for the first time he stopped looking jaundiced.

To himself he breathed, 'Now, that was smart work. These Feds sure know what to do, I'll hand it to them.' Suspecting everyone they were, slickly looking for clues right from the word 'Go.' Not even excluding from their suspicions this old man who was reporting the crime. And the gangling, straw-haired G-man with the nickname of Pavlova took up the trail the moment the old man sat beside him. G-man Sorensen leaned over from the back and listened.

They shot up the winding lane, the police car coming quickly after them, Pavlova said, casually, 'You went to borrow a cart, you said?'

The old man chewed his gums then said, 'Nope. I went to borry a lead horse.

66

I ain't got a lead horse so I have to borry from Cal when I want one.'

Pavlova tried again. 'And Cal, you say, had had his head beaten in with a stick?'

Joe ruminated, then said, 'Nope, Cal's lyin' there with the flies buzzin' round him. His head's smashed in, but I don't reckon to know what with. I just ran into the house, saw Edie — that's Cal's wife — lyin' there, so I went right back and got my car headed for the police.'

Sorensen unobtrusively tapped the G-man driver on the shoulder. It meant, 'Lay off. He doesn't depart from his original story. Maybe he's on the level.' But all people at all times are suspect to G-men when they are called in on a crime. Old Joe Finney would continue to be a suspect until the F.B.I. records called this case closed.

Joe turned them into a farm track and they bumped their way up and over a hill and then abruptly came into the farm-yard.

It was a typical small Virginia home-stead, with a farmhouse that had started as a timber dwelling but had had a brick section added to it. It was set back among some protective trees, through which came a glimpse of long low-roofed farm buildings. On the open side were fields that looked to be well-tilled and tended. Right in front of the shapeless old farmhouse was a yard in which some derelict farm wagons lay rotting at one side, and a shed with an open door that probably served as a garage. Grass grew between the stones that had been hammered into the ground to serve as an approach to the front door of the farmstead, and some hens were scratching in dusty hollows close by the inevitable manure heap.

'There,' said Joe, as the car pulled up. He pointed towards the hut with the open door. Someone was lying face downwards.

The police car came in behind them, and all five walked across to look at the remains of Cal Turner. He was roughly dressed in much the manner of his neighbour, Joe Finney, though he was a bigger man, more powerfully made. There wasn't much to be seen of his head for the congealed blood that was on it. They didn't need to investigate further to see that he was most certainly dead.

Lief Sorensen looked quickly at a mess of tyre tracks that covered the ground hereabouts, then strode off towards the house. Old Joe stayed outside this time. He said he didn't want to see any more, and the old man looked suddenly sick.

The other four went through the open door. They went into the farm living room — low-raftered, furnished with wheel-backed chairs, a rocker, an old horsehair couch with the stuffing showing at the worn end, and a plain white-scrubbed table. A roughly furnished room, such as you would expect in these parts.

And on the floor was Edie Turner, wife of Cal Turner, deceased — and herself very much deceased.

The floor was stone paved. Sorensen held the others back a second while he looked down for scratch marks. He saw them — plenty. Then remembered the heavy farm boots on the corpse outside.

They went across to the second victim.

Her long dark hair was wild over her face, staring sightlessly upwards. Her head lay in a pool of dark blood, and they guessed she had been hit hard also. Over on the floor was a heavy poker that would normally have been in the fire grate.

The G-man and the two police looked at the woman and understood what old Joe Finney had meant when he said: '. . . someone hadn't bin nice to her afore she died.'

Sorensen immediately went out to where old Joe Finney was standing with his battered hat held in his long, stringy hand. He said, 'Joe, that hut looks like a garage to me, but I don't see no car. Did Cal have one?'

Joe said, 'A sedan, an old one. He traded it last year fer a blamed ol' thing that kept breakin' down — '

Sorensen said, 'Sure, Joe, but do you remember the number?'

Joe kept thinking for a long time then said, apologetically, 'I seen that car almost every day, but I guess I never thought to remember the number.'

Sorensen wasn't put out. 'Records'll

have it, sergeant. Get through on your radio and report this crime. Have records chase up the registration number of Cal Turner's sedan, and have an all-roads watch put out for that car. Tell them the occupants will probably — but not certainly — be two escaped convicts from North Carolina, by name Ernst Schiller and Johnny Delcros. Schiller can be easily recognised — he hasn't a hair on his head.'

The patrolman, not the sergeant, went across to his car and started up the radio. The sergeant said, 'What makes you so sure it's Schiller and Delcros done this? To date you've only some scratch marks on a brake pedal to tell you things. Could be this was done by a lot of other people.'

Pavlova's straw hair came up. He didn't say anything but his eyes said to Sorensen, 'The hell, these cops don't always have to act so jealous of the F.B.I., do they?'

Sorensen was thinking of other things, and was inclined to be abrupt now. 'You should look into the fireplace. It's a hot day, yet someone's had a fire. And in the

71

grate is a pile of charred matter, which I'll guess is the remains of prison issue clothing. Go get samples for the Bureau backroom boys, Pav.'

He hunted around for clues for a time, then said, 'I don't think we can do much more here, sergeant. You stay until the Criminal Investigation people arrive to fingerprint things. We're going back to H.Q. so's to be on hand when any further news comes through. Come on, Pav.'

The sergeant said one more thing. 'I ain't never heard of a man called Pavlova before.'

Big Sorensen lifted one eyebrow and looked at his gangling companion. 'There's a story behind that,' he said. 'You should ask him for it someday.' They all looked at the G-man known as Pavlova, who went uncomfortable and seemed ashamed about something.

Then Sorensen got into the car, taking the wheel, and his companion hunched beside him and said, sourly, 'You didn't ought to make a fool of me like that, Lief.'

And then he sat and grumbled until

Sorensen interrupted, 'You know how I see it?'

Pavlova said, 'They needed clothes and food and money. They picked on this farmhouse because it was off the main road and lonely. They found the wife alone.' He paused. 'They're a low type, and they've been kept from women for a few years.'

He was no fool, the G-man with the freckles. Sorensen turned on to the better road and opened out. He ended the story for his companion.

'Yeah, and maybe the husband wasn't so far away and heard her screaming. He came back and they saw him coming and went out and hit him until he dropped. These boys are pretty desperate. Then they went back — and finished the wife because they reckoned she'd be too dangerous a witness to leave alive. Then they got whatever clothes they could find, burned their own, took food and any money they could see, and went off in Cal Turner's sedan.'

Pavlova found a cigarette and lit it. Sorensen didn't smoke. Pavlova said, 'It's nearly always the same. When there's a jailbreak, they hop from place to place in one stolen car after another. At some place they meet resistance and they get tough and kill someone. Then we or the police are called in to clean up the mess, find the birds and get them back in the pen.'

Sorensen said, 'These birds won't live long in the pen once we get them there.'

They got back to the F.B.I. field office. News was chattering in on the teleprinter. Someone said, 'This is for you, Lief,' and he bent over the glass top to see what was coming up.

It said, 'Cal Turner's car reported in accident at Rime End, North Carolina. Occupants got out, held up another car and forced the driver to drive them away.' More details followed.

Lief looked at the big wall map and said, 'Now, what in hell . . . They come all this way out of North Carolina and now they're doubling right back on their tracks. Can you think of a reason, Pav?'

Pavlova thought and said, 'I could think of a million.'

He didn't know he was exactly right.

# 5

Warren Bridge — 23 miles

Johnny got into the sedan with that lifeless body only a few yards away, and at once headed south, back the way they had just come. Their plans were made, and they didn't need to talk about them.

They had driven north — and Petersburg, Washington and that paradise and hiding place of criminals New York, were all north of North Carolina — in an attempt to lead a blind trail. The idea now was to run along the border until they reached Kentucky and then strike north for the big industrial city of Cincinatti.

Somewhere en route they would stop and burn this old sedan so as to it render identification difficult if not impossible. Other 'borrowed' vehicles would get them to Cincinnati. And in that city was a girlfriend of Johnny's, a girl who would be willing to hide them until the heat went off.

But their plans didn't run quite so smoothly.

There were times when the border road crossed into North Carolina territory, and they were in one such place when they crashed into another car. It was just after they'd stopped at an isolated filling station.

Johnny was speculating on the possible connection of their escape with the couple of stiffs back at the farm. Thick-eared, heavy-browed Johnny liked to speculate, but it just annoyed the more silent, sombre Egghead.

He was saying, 'Maybe they won't think about us. I mean, how'n Hades can they connect us? We wiped down the coupé so there wouldn't be no fingerprints, an' we croaked the dame because she was the only one saw us. I mean, how'n hell can the cops wise up to us?'

Egghead said, 'Lord knows, but cops do things you don't expect. As for the Feds . . . ' And then he said, sourly, 'Look where you're goin'. You're travellin' fast fer an old car.'

At which moment a spanking new sedan came shooting out of a side road, and Johnny ran slap into it because he found the brakes were suddenly not working so good.

Nobody got hurt, but there was an awful lot of glass and bent metal around the place, and the owner of the new car looked fit to cry any moment. He was trying to blame Johnny and Egghead, but for once they were virtuously free from error and were able to snarl back at him better than he gave.

But the pair were jumpy. This put an end to the idea of burning the farmer's car and so abruptly hiding their tracks. Johnny hadn't time for that, and that meant they would have to leave it and the cops would come along in time and know that the killers of the farm couple were heading south-west again.

Johnny started swearing, but Egghead snarled for him to shut his mouth. The gink in the new car might hear too much. At which moment a powerful sedan came pulling up at sight of an interesting smash.

Egghead ran across and got in the way so that the fellow had to stop completely. He didn't look pleased. He wore a loud tie and had a voice to match. Egghead thought he might be some local big shot who didn't like rough farm-working types to tell him what to do.

Egghead began, 'We need your car.'

The tie looked at Egghead's dirty jeans and said, 'You can need. This car don't carry tramps, and I'm in a hurry.'

Egghead said, dispassionately, 'I ain't no tramp, and something here says you'd better not try movin'.'

The tie looked up and saw a gun in Egghead's hand. For a moment he seemed too startled to understand. In that moment the gink in the wrecked car saw the gun and let out a squawk. Johnny promptly pulled a gun on him.

Egghead called, 'Climb in, Johnny,' and covered the driver until Johnny had backed into the big car. Johnny would have liked to have gone through the gink's pockets, but they were afraid every minute that other traffic would come along.

Egghead got in beside the driver and ordered, 'Get up that road, fast,' and obediently the man with the tie that was loud even in a land of loud ties stepped on the gas.

Five miles along they stopped an approaching car — a fast Buick — took the clothes off both drivers, tied them and shoved them into the back of the powerful sedan. This they drove into some bushes. If the gink back in his battered auto had had the sense to take the number of the sedan, this manoeuvre would break the trail.

But not for long.

Johnny voiced the thought. Egghead was driving this time, and Johnny was trying to put on a loud, hand-painted tie in a swaying, fast-speeding auto. The clothes didn't fit either of them, but there had been plenty of money in the pockets.

Johnny said, 'They'll find that sedan with them guys before dark, you bet. The cops move fast when they're told there's guys around totin' guns at motorists.'

Egghead grunted. Johnny went on, 'They'll have roadblocks everywhere, then, knowing we'll have taken another car. Maybe we should have croaked the fellar that owned this, so's to keep his mouth shut about the registration number.'

Egghead started to slow down. What Johnny was saying seemed good guesswork. He pulled up. 'Looks like we'll never make Kentucky, you reckon, Johnny?'

Johnny kept watch back up the road. 'I figger we should hide out now, Eggy. Hittin' that blasted car's upset everything. If they put roadblocks out everywhere it doesn't matter how many cars you swap, they're bound to stop you sometime.' He looked at his companion's head, hidden under a hat that was too small for him. 'And you're conspicuous, Eggy.' He said 'conspishus', but Egghead knew what he meant.

Egghead was touchy about his lack of hair and scowled. All the same, there was no arguing against what Johnny was saying. Their plans hadn't worked out right, and now they must make others quickly.

Egghead said, 'I don't know this country.'

Johnny said, 'Neither do I. Reckon we can't be far from Tennessee.' He was looking at the sign at a fork. The light wasn't too good in this wooded defile, with the sun already down behind the hill. 'But I guess we gotta find some place, someone who'll look after us.'

He said, suddenly, 'I'm goin' across to that sign. I've got an idea it says somethin' interestin'.'

He looked back again quickly, then got out and hurried over the road. He didn't actually reach the sign, then turned and ran back.

Egghead, curious, said, 'What is it? You found somethin'?'

Johnny got in, said, 'Turn south down that fork road.'

Egghead didn't argue; he put the car in gear and pulled across the road. As they passed under the sign he read. 'Warren Bridge — 23 miles.'

Egghead opened up, remarking, 'You know someone in Warren Bridge?'

'We both do.' The light was fading

rapidly, and Egghead switched on the headlights. Johnny said, 'I was tellin' you, back by the gas chamber in Halifax. Old Rocky lived at Warren Bridge, once — his brother lives there now.'

Egghead said, 'So what?' but he was thinking of something that Rocky had said to Johnny, something about his brother sitting on a stolen million.

'So,' said Johnny, grimly, 'we look up this brother and we tell him we want to stay with him for a week or two, see? Maybe when he knows we're from his brother in jail he'll be helpful, huh? Maybe that guy'll have a conscience because of what he's done to old Rocky.'

Egghead grunted a doubtful, 'Maybe.'

So Johnny turned and said, 'He won't want trouble if what Rocky told me is right — about both of them being in that big fraud racket, but only Rocky took the rap. Okay, so maybe he'll be agreeable to us hiding out with him for a time.'

Egghead said, 'We ain't got much option, Johnny, I guess we'd better get somewhere out of sight quick. An' Rocky's brother sounds something like a safe bet. But we gotta find that out.'

He gave the car the gun and they rocked through the gathering dusk. After a while Johnny switched on the radio and dialled for music. Egghead spoke above it. 'You said something about a million being stashed away?'

Johnny said, 'That might be an old man's hokum. He used to say they'd cleaned up a million with company frauds, and it was all baked away. He said his brother was takin' care of it until he'd served his sentence. But I wouldn't know. These old men get to sayin' big things and next is they're believin' them themselves. Maybe we'll find there ain't no million, only a coupla hundred bucks or so.'

Egghead drove for a while in silence, and then he said what Johnny was thinking. 'Old Rocky must have been near on seventy when they gave him his sentence. It was a ten-year rap, yeah?' Johnny nodded, his brow furrowing because he was pursuing the same thought.

Egghead said, 'Judges, they're all

buzzards, but they don't give ten-year sentences to old men unless they've pulled off somethin' really big.'

They were approaching the outskirts of a fair-sized town now. They guessed it to be Warren Bridge. Egghead eased off, but still let the headlights slice into the darkness against the thickening oncoming traffic.

He continued, 'It could be that old Rocky ain't dreamin'. Could be that he cleaned up a million an' left it with his brother. That's a good reason why we should call on Rocky's brother.'

Johnny said, 'Sure, it's a million good reasons. And maybe we c'n step in an' protect old Rocky's interests for him, huh?'

Egghead let his tight face slip into an appreciative smile at that. 'Maybe we might, Johnny,' he said. And he was thinking that two into one million spoilt a nice round figure

Johnny was grinning. 'It might be a good hideout at that, Eggy,' he said, and he was watching his companion out of the corner of his eye. He had an idea what

Egghead was thinking, so he switched his mind to the same thought. He had been backward at school and never seemed to learn how to make two go into anything — certainly not a million.

The music stopped. Music always stops when you switch on a radio. It was a local station, and it came out with a news bulletin.

So, being a local station, it put local news before the war at the other end of the world, the political racket in Washington, and a catastrophe in Northern India.

Egghead and Johnny heard the cultivated excitement of the announcer as he raced through his opening spiel — 'Today there was a daring double break from the jail at Halifax, N.C. Two prisoners got away in a laundry truck. Then, later, two more prisoners broke out over the wall.'

Egghead's bald head came round in astonishment. 'What — ?' he began, then shut up as the announcer rattled on.

'The second jailbreak was a spectacular affair. Five members of the old Savannah mob that used to terrorise the western territory of our state made a break for it.

Three were armed with guns, and the other two grabbed weapons from guards when the break began. Two men were shot down as they tried to get over the wall. Three escaped, but one broke an ankle in dropping from the wall, and is now in hospital. Three guards were hurt in the fighting, one seriously.

'The men who escaped are well-known mobsters. Their names? Jud Corbeta and Joe Guestler.'

Johnny started swearing softly, but there was more to come.

'The prisoners were last heard of heading west towards the Warren Bridge district. A watch is being kept on all roads . . . '

Johnny snapped off the radio. 'The hell,' he snarled. 'Guestler and Corbeta. They musta got mad 'cause we beat 'em to it, and they went through with their old plan.'

Egghead growled, 'Yeah, but how come they're heading right where we are now — Warren Bridge?'

Johnny opened his mouth and then shut it. A powerful car had raced up from behind and was now forcing them to the side of the street. It was a shopping centre, and there were a lot of people about.

Egghead started snarling, and then Johnny got what he was saying.

It was a police car.

# 6

## Bronya Karkoff

The chief got Sorensen and his assistant up in his office. He was another of Edgar Hoover's bright young men, full of ideas and energy. He said, 'The F.B.I. have taken over this case, Sorensen. It's yours to direct, so get out and direct it. First, though, there's all the information we have to date to help you.

'That stolen cream coupé that came from near Halifax, North Carolina. There are no fingerprints anywhere on it.'

Lief said, 'So we don't know if it was Schiller and Delcros who took it. It could have been anyone.'

The chief nodded. 'Could be. We won't think either way. Just go out and follow every clue. However, it's still a good guess that whoever stole the coupé is connected with that double farmhouse killing.' He paused. 'Killing that woman suggests very desperate men — you know what I mean, hungry. Could be men, for instance, who have been shut off for several years from contact with women.'

'Which gives a hint that it might still be our escaped convict friends,' Sorensen nodded. Pavlova said nothing but he was following everything alertly. The chief went on:

'I received a phone call from Rime End just before you came in. The local police say there are no prints on that car, either — the murdered farmer's sedan. So we don't know if the murder connects up with the jailbreak.' The chief fingered a message form. 'I don't know whether this has any connection with the case. A report came in to say that just outside Rime End is a lonely filling station. A girl in charge was held up by a couple of — she calls them farm workers. They locked her in a room, took all the loose money, and went off after filling up their car with gas. I'd say you should call in on the girl as you go through, and see what leads she can give you. Her name's Bronya Karkoff; she's a medical student working her way through college.'

Pavlova jotted the name down, along with the address of the filling station.

The chief said, 'Now, about the last thing to tell you. You may have heard that after Schiller and Delcros got away, later that day there was a very deliberate escape bid on the part of another group of prisoners, They are reported to be some of the old Savannah gang boys, who played hell up and down the coast towns for years, remember?'

Sorensen did remember. 'It was before my time in the F.B.I, but the papers gave them plenty of space and I could read. I guess they're pretty tough, those boys . . . Who got away?'

'Joe Guestler and Jud Corbeta. A nice pair of lice. Louie Savannah got over the wall but bust his ankle when he made the drop. Those three had automatics, and they were using them. We still don't know how they got them smuggled into jail. Guestler and Corbeta held up a car outside, hit the driver over the head and drove off. They swapped cars a few times, then we lost the trail. Last seen, though, they were heading in the general direction of Kansey Cross, Old Ford, Warren Bridge and places west. The police threw a cordon out immediately, and they say it is unlikely that the pair could have got beyond Warren Bridge.'

Sorensen studied for a moment. 'You think maybe the two escape bids are related, and both pairs of convicts are rendezvousing at Warren Bridge?'

The chief smiled. 'I'm not making any suggestions. It is a possibility and one you should bear in mind, but remember not to start making evidence fit a theory — just go and dig up all the clues you can and see what answer they give.'

It was a warning delivered time and again to field operators of the F.B.I,, but the chief didn't think that Sorensen would need it . . . Lief Sorensen was a very level, very able man, and hadn't fallen down on a case yet.

Sorensen said, 'It'll be dark soon. I think we'll start off for Rime End immediately. We'll call in on that girl with the Russian name on our way.'

'And then?' asked the chief.

'I think we'll go on to Warren Bridge. That is, unless something else turns up meanwhile. We'll take a radio car.'

The chief nodded, rising. 'You'll find the Warren Bridge chief of police to be a cooperative man. Unlike some police chiefs he doesn't get jealous of the F.B.I. and become obstructive. Give him my regards, will you?'

They went out.

Nearly an hour later they pulled up at a small filling station just on the outskirts of Rime End. A girl in a white monkey suit stood and watched suspiciously as they got out of the car. Maybe she was allergic to bulky men who got out of sedans when there was no other car traffic about.

Sorensen came up and said, humorously, 'You can take your hand off that monkey-wrench; we wouldn't like a monkey-wrench wrapped round our pretty heads, would we Pav?'

The girl put the wrench on to an oil-soaked workbench. She sighed audibly, and her relief was apparent.

She was a good-looker, with dark, glossy hair that picked up all the stray lights and reflected them, and a face that was high-cheekboned, giving her a piquant, foreign expression. That was the Russian in her, Sorensen thought. He was young enough to appreciate a good-looking girl. He waited for her voice, and hoped he wouldn't be disappointed. He wasn't.

When she spoke she had a good, level, educated way of speaking, and she sounded intelligent. Sorensen thought she would have to be intelligent, to be studying for a degree in medicine.

'I'm glad to see you,' she said. 'You'll be the F.B.I, I suppose? I was warned to stay until you arrived.'

She looked at the gathering darkness and shuddered. 'I wasn't going to stay much longer, though. I've had enough of this place — and not just for tonight, either!'

'Quitting?'

She nodded emphatically. She had brown eyes, Sorensen saw; very dark, almost black in the fading light. 'Yes, this place is too lonely. I'll get a vacation job some place else, I guess.'

They walked into the lighted office, the usual small place with tyre advertisements, cardboard plug cutouts, and greasy oil charts on the wall. One small desk under the window, a couple of uncertain chairs and a spike for bills seemed to be the only furniture.

The girl continued, 'I've been here three weeks. It's surprising how much trade this little place gets. But sometimes, when things are quiet, the odd he-man rolls up and makes a pass at me. That's why I keep that monkey-wrench handy. It always works with wolves.'

'But not farmhands?' said Sorensen gently.

Bronya's head shook vigorously. She shuddered, remembering. 'They didn't look wolves. Wolves mostly drive around in big cars with tooting horns; these came in the sort of old wagon you'd expect with farm workers.'

'What was it like?' Pavlova, taking down the details, came up with the question. Bronya looked at him, with his bony wrists and big red hands and straw thatch atop a red, freckled face. He didn't look like a G-man, but all the same he seemed a good sort.

She said, disappointingly, 'I don't remember. Just that it was a sedan and pretty shabby. I couldn't say what colour it was, either. You see, you get into the habit of looking at your customers, not their car, first thing when they drive in.

'Well, these didn't give me much chance to look at them long. They came across to where I was standing at the pump. Both looked round quickly, then they grabbed me and shoved me inside this office. I shouted, and one of the pair gave me a backhander that knocked me down. I suppose I was dazed. When I began to get my wits together again they'd helped themselves to the day's takings. Then they shoved me into the closet there, and locked the door on me. It's dark, and there's no other way out of that place. I just stood quite quietly and heard them fill up and then drive off. Some time later I heard someone drive in, and I started hollering and banging on the door with my fists and feet. The driver heard me, and I shouted instructions to him, but he was a dumb cluck and didn't seem to understand, for he drove away.'

Sorensen said, 'Maybe he wasn't so dumb. Maybe he took fright at sight of a robbed till. Maybe he has a record and didn't want to be connected any way with a hold-up that hadn't brought him any profit.'

Bronya said, 'Maybe. Well, the next guy that came along was a truck driver with blood in his veins. He couldn't be bothered to find a lever to force the lock, he just set to and kicked the door down.'

Pavlova said, drily, 'Truck drivers are like that. Men of simple habits.' And then he said, 'Try to describe the men to me, please, Miss Karkoff.'

Again she shrugged helplessly. 'It happened so quickly, I don't remember much. They were pretty big, both of them. Maybe not as big as you two, but nearing the six-foot mark. And both were lean men, the kind you expect in farm clothes. They both wore old cloth caps, and they were pulled well down over their heads.'

Pavlova sighed. 'So you wouldn't be

able to say if one was as bald as a barrel of lard, huh?'

Bronya shook her head. She got nicer, the more you looked at her. For now she was peeling off the monkey-suit, and the more she peeled, the nicer she looked.

Out of the suit she had long legs, and long-legged girls have *It* where men are concerned. They were bare and well-muscled and in her sandalled feet she looked athletic. The effect was heightened by her college shorts, with a monogram in maroon, stitched against the saxe blue of one leg. A neat, cream linen blouse completed her attire. It made her look seventeen. In fact she was over twenty.

Pavlova said, 'You didn't answer me,' looking at those long bare legs as she rolled up her monkey-suit and tucked it into a locker.

Bronya said, 'They weren't gentlemen; they kept their hats on in my presence, so I wouldn't know.' She added, 'And I got my long legs so that I could hurdle at college. You like 'em?'

She sounded a mite aggressive, and Pavolva curled up inside his notebook.

Big Sorensen grinned and relieved his companion by saying, 'Could you recognize them again, Miss Karkoff?'

'Maybe.' She was very uncertain. 'They'd dirtied their faces, so it would be difficult,' She frowned with annoyance and then said frankly, 'I'm not being very helpful, am I? But men who come with the idea of sticking up a lonely garage don't usually give you much chance to see things, and I guess that clip across the face didn't clear my brain much.'

Sorensen said, consolingly, 'That's all right, Miss Karkoff. We didn't expect much more. I'm sorry you had such a bad experience.'

He was thinking to himself: Maybe you were lucky at that. If the farmhands were our escaped convicts, it's a good job for you that you were the second woman they met in their freedom, not the first. He was thinking of how that woman had looked up at the farm. Then he looked at the nice, slim girl before him and tried not to think of what could have happened to her.

Bronya slipped on a small jacket. It

made her look older. Now she looked quite seventeen and a half, thought Sorensen. She said, 'I'm supposed to stay on till ten, then the boss comes for the money and gives me a lift back into Warren Bridge. He's got a lot of filling stations in this county.'

'But you don't feel like waiting for him?'

'He can jump in the lake,' she said determinedly. 'A nice polluted lake, too. He shouldn't have girls out at lonely places like this. Something's bound to happen, sometime; I can see that now. If you're going Warren Bridge way . . . '

Sorensen said, 'The way you say it, Miss Karkoff, I couldn't help but go to Warren Bridge. Sure we'll take you.'

She liked that little humorous way he had of saying things. He was a big, reassuring man, this Fed, and just now she had need for reassuring men around her. She said, demurely, 'That'll be fine. But you make me sound like a town in Russia, with all this 'Miss Karkoffing'. I answer better to Bronya.'

Sorensen said, 'I answer to a lot of names.'

'Such as?'

'Honey-bunch, cutie-pie, sugar, darling — and Lief Sorensen.'

'We'll start backwards,' said the girl, and her eyes were dancing. 'Lief Sorensen now, and maybe the rest to follow.'

Lief said, 'Could be just right at that.'

Pavlova sighed and closed his book. 'Guess my presence is embarrassing to you. Must be tough, making up with a gooseberry round about. Things go so slow, don't they?'

They looked at him kindly. Bronya said, 'All men want all women. All men, if they aren't freaks, get jealous if they think they're losing ground with a girl.' She added, 'We learn that sort of stuff in our medical studies nowadays. It comes in very useful.'

Lief said, 'You don't have to take it to heart, Pavlova. When you're a big, big man, maybe the girls will play with you, too.'

They were all kidding, and it was good fun. They went outside and the girl looked up. It was so dark now that Lief had to use a torch to examine for tyre tracks and footmarks on the oily concrete front. He said, 'We'll be better getting on to Warren Bridge. It seems pretty certain that the car was Cal Turner's.'

The girl said, 'Was?' She was climbing into the back of the car; Pavlova was behind the wheel, starting the engine. Lief hesitated, not sure which seat to occupy.

He found himself saying, 'Yeah, was. Those men who held you up killed him a few hours back — and killed his wife, too.'

From the darkness of the car he heard her draw in a long breath that seemed to saw into her lungs. Then she released it and it came out in just the same irregular fashion. He said, quickly, 'You all right?' But he knew she wasn't.

He heard her whisper, 'Come and sit beside me, Lief. I — I feel all tuckered in. I knew all the time those men were really bad . . . '

He got in and closed the door. Pavlova sat stiff behind the wheel. He was jealous. He was an F.B.I. man but he was also twenty-four. And at twenty-four you don't like to drive a car with another couple right behind you in the dark.

Lief could feel the girl trembling. He knew that the joking back at the filling-station had been a front, knew now that the fright the girl had got had been near to breaking her up, and now reaction was setting in.

He sat next to her, not attempting to touch her. You never knew with a highly-strung girl how she might take even a little pat of consolation.

So she came up against him, said, 'I knew they'd killed somebody. I don't know how I knew. They didn't speak a word, and there wasn't — ' she shuddered — 'blood on their clothes. But — oh, God, I knew it, somehow! Knew they'd done something dreadful like murder. It was in their eyes . . . '

Lief said, immediately, 'What colour were they?'

And the girl sobbed, 'For God's sake don't be an F.B.I. man now, Lief. I'm — I'm scared to death, still. I don't know how I waited there all that time for police and then you.' He could hear her teeth chattering. She crept closer up to him; he felt her take his hand and put it round her shoulders. They were heaving.

She said, crying, 'Just let me think you're my daddy for a few minutes, Lief. I — I feel awful bad.'

There was nothing to see, through Rime and where the Turner car had crashed into another auto. They had had to clear the road for traffic, and now the wrecked cars had been towed away. Pavlova sent the big car leaping towards distant Warren Bridge.

They came to it around ten o'clock. As they drove in they saw an ambulance screaming away down a side street. A few seconds later two more flashed towards them, and turned down the same street. Then apparently the entire town's fire appliances came clanging down, with police cars and another ambulance in between.

Lief sat up, said, 'Something pretty big seems to have broken in Warren Bridge tonight. Now I wonder what it could be?'

Pavlova's rusty voice came back to him. 'Wonder if it's got anything to do with our convict friends?'

Sorensen ordered, 'We'll go back and see, Pavlova.'

And the driver at once turned and followed the shrilling, sirening, bell-clanging procession.

Bronya asked, 'It's a queer name for a man to have — Pavlova.' She was feeling better now. Lief could feel her tidying her hair and then came the nose-tingling dusty scent as she flopped a powder-puff across her face.

The G-man driver heard. He growled, 'Okay it's a queer name, but I didn't ask for it. A lotta wise guys gave it me. They've put my name down on the roll as Ben Arcota, but nobody don't ever call me that now.'

They turned down the side street. It opened on to a shopping promenade, all very new and dazzling with its electric signs. They had to stop, because of the big crowd that choked the end of the square. Pavlova pulled in to the sidewalk and they got out.

Lief said, 'Are you staying in the car?' But the girl shook her head and the three went into the square together. Pavlova, ahead, kept saying, 'Make way there, police,' and in time they came out through a cordon of patrolmen into the open.

There were flowerbeds and trees all down the middle of the square. They could see them plainly because of spotlights from police cars and the fire appliances, which were trained on the square and lighting it up with astonishing brilliance.

The lights seemed to converge on a spot opposite where neons proclaimed a movie-house — the Southern Star.

Hurrying across, Sorensen exclaimed, 'My God, what's happened? An earthquake?'

There was a lot of noise as they came up to the crowd of people working outside the movie-house. A lot of crying, a lot of hysterics from women, and an awful lot of moaning as of people in pain.

They saw that men were going into the Southern Star and coming out carrying injured people, all around stretcher bearers were loading up the ambulances and dispatching them in relays to the hospital.

Sorensen saw a big car parked on the roadside by the Southern Star. In the brilliant lights he read the chief of police's sign and went across. The patrolman at the wheel pointed out the chief, standing supervising the evacuation of the building, and they went across to him and introduced themselves.

Sorensen said, 'This is probably none of our business.'

The chief rapped, 'I don't know. Five people were killed in that awful stampede. Four were trampled to death, three being women. One seems to have died from heart failure.'

Sorensen, Ben Arcota and Bronya looked at the crowded cinema front, with people lying all around on the grass verge.

Sorensen asked, 'What caused the stampede, chief?'

The chief spat. He said, enigmatically, 'The Conscience of America.'

# 7

## Stampede

Patrolman Luke Campion was torn between two signs. One said, 'Iced Beer — It's cooling, this weather'. The other carried a similar appeal — 'It's cooler inside'.

Luke worked it out. And the three hours of coolness within the Southern Star won. For the price of three cool hours was roughly the price of one pint of cool beer which wouldn't last three minutes in Luke's present overheated state.

So — off duty that fateful night, he planked a dollar down at the cash desk, took his change and went inside.

It was cool. That was about the only thing good he could say about the programme. There was a crime film on and it bore no resemblance to anything he had ever met up with in his police life.

The crooks looked so much like crooks they'd never have been allowed a life outside a prison cell, the police were all flat-faced morons who were there to make the patrons laugh, and the hero did things that were in defiance of all the legal codes in any state in the U.S.

He sat and chewed a cigarette and wished he'd picked a musical. Something with legs. Legs could make up for a lot of story deficiencies.

The film came to an end in time, and then the screen went white and nothing else happened. The house was packed with patrons here to escape the oppressive heat of the evening, and after a few minutes they began to get restless. Luke wasn't bothered and didn't think anything about it, but then he wasn't what you might call a film fan. In fact he thought it was pleasanter to sit in the cool without the distraction of some inanity on the screen before him.

A picture began to screen. There was something curious about it. It didn't have any intro wording, didn't seem to have been edited in any way, and there was no sound attached to the screening.

It all seemed like one of the old silent film dramas, to most of the audience.

They saw a clearing among stunted trees, with cars parked in a crescent beneath them. Men were standing around among the cars and you could see them drinking.

Luke thought: 'It's gonna be a plug for somebody's summer drinks. Maybe Coca-cola.'

But the filming didn't concentrate on the men drinking. Instead they saw a group of men, apart by a very big car, hoist something upright. It was a man, bound and gagged. They saw the rope around his legs being unfastened and then the man was roughly shoved towards a solitary tree.

Then came an incident when a little man separated from the throng and knocked the bound man about a bit. There was a startled gasp from the audience, and Luke Campion sat up; for the little man had turned at one point and seemed to be talking straight into the camera and there wasn't any doubt as to his identity.

'Skidmore,' people whispered one to the other, astonished. 'Elmer Skidmore, of the Skidmore grocery chain!' And then they asked, 'What'n heck's all this about?' And because the film was silent they were able to speculate aloud.

They saw the man roughly — unnecessarily roughly — bound to a tree, and then another gasp went up as a big, heavy-limbed man came prominently into the picture.

For they recognised this man, too.

It was Frank Descoign; and Frank Descoign owned the Southern Star and all the other Star cinemas along this Virginia-North Carolina border, and one or two in Old Kentucky also.

They saw Frank shouting soundlessly, then going away, to return with a gasoline can. Then a shocked, 'Ooooh!' came from the audience as the silent Frank swung back the can and swooshed the contents over the bound man before him, and they saw the toothless mouth open in an inaudible scream of pain as the searing gasoline bit deep into tender eyes.

It was at this moment that Luke

Campion and most of the audience got an idea — an idea that this was no playacting they were watching, no trick of photography, but something real.

The torment and torture of a fellow human being.

And they were having to sit there and watch and not be able to help the sufferer; because all this had happened, this they were seeing was only a record of what had been. Whatever tragedy had occurred, had happened and was over.

As realization came, men began to shout in anger, and then women's voices were raised and with them the frightened cries of a few up-late children. Women were rising, starting to move along the rows of seats, not wanting to see any more.

Because all knew what was to come, because this wasn't the first time in the history of the Old North State that a man had been burned at a stake.

And still the film unreeled, steadily, remorselessly, a cold objective record of what had happened in that glade of oaks.

They saw Frank Descoign, waddling forward cautiously on bloated limbs, tossing a lighted match on to the grass before the victim. Nothing, for a second, and in that time part of the audience prayed that nothing would happen, while in the hearts of some was a momentary disappointment.

Then a pillar of fire stemmed up, reaching out to embrace the figure held against the tree, and clearly they saw that last agony of the victim. And saw the sadistic glee on so many faces that they recognized, now that a greater light shone on them.

Besides Descoign and Skidmore were Ben Tavistock, who had several tailoring establishments, Gowiddis the big dry-cleaner, Rubbold an architect, and Tom Dryway and Geordie Humble, who were partners in an expanding chemical industry. There was someone who looked like Arthur Hepburn, the tractor agent, Arthur Whitwam who had the big canning concern, and Mancini and the drug store monopolist.

And others.

Then the amplifier came alive, and over the sound of shouting and hysteria they heard a voice boom, 'This is the Conscience of America speaking. Let it look upon these things, and let it shout aloud in protest. You who sit there — are you going to let these miscreants free to do this all over again? Will you go away and say nothing? Or will you demand the extreme penalty for the murderers of this unfortunate citizen of our great and glorious country?'

And then the fool at the microphone began to shout, 'Death, death! Let death be the lot of these criminals. Death, death! As they have done unto this man, let it be done unto them. This is the Conscience of America demanding . . . Death for the killers, death for the murderers, death . . . '

No one heard the rest of the hysterical demand for retribution. The place was in a panic and an uproar. The film was still screening, so that they could see the last fearful agony, and it was too much for most of the women and many of the men, too.

All at once a lot of people were trying to get out of the cinema, and within seconds the movement had assumed the proportions of an uncontrollable panic. Between the seats was a claustrophobic shamble of struggling, hysterical people; out on the aisles was a locked mass who became claustrophobic because of the pressure one upon the other, and who struggled and lashed out in an effort to extricate themselves. In the press a few fell and couldn't rise and were trampled on by hundreds of milling, stamping feet.

And still the film silently projected light and shadows on to that big silver screen, so that they saw the throwing of the gasoline can, the explosion and the momentary panic of the lynchers that followed, and then the collapsing of the charred hulk of a man face down among the burning grass.

Luke Campion with other men shouted for people to stay where they were; but in the frenzied excitement no one heard them and the panic went on. Campion saw that he could do nothing for the moment, and he kept his wits about him.

He walked along the tops of the rows of seats to the back of the hall; after a short struggle he got out of the mad mass of fighting people and went up the stairs to the projection room. The door opened to his touch. Two men lay on the floor.

Luke went across to the men. They were bound and gagged, adhesive tape having been used for both purposes. He pulled out a knife and slit through the gags, then pulled them off. Both men came out swearing at the loss of hair from their cheeks. Then there was more swearing as the tape was unwound from their wrists. They went on swearing a long time after they were free and on their feet. They were youngish men and full of heat at the discomfort and indignity of their recent position.

Luke gave them half a minute and then said, 'Okay, this is where I came in. Now let's be knowing what happened to you.'

One said, 'Nothing much, Suddenly a lot of fellars came in and grabbed us and tied us up. Then they put a film on, and one of the guys with a neck like a turkey's started spieling into the mike.'

'You heard what he said?'

'You can't hear, not lying where we were on the floor. The shutter drowned the noise.'

Campion told them what he'd heard and what had happened in the hall. Then he went out and for a while gave a hand at carrying out injured and fainted people. When he saw the flood of relief workers come pouring in he left off and went in search of the chief. He found him with a couple of big men and a very pretty girl across on the grass verge where the injured were lying.

Campion saluted automatically, though he was off duty and in civvies. He said, 'I was inside, sir. Do you want my report?'

The chief grabbed him. He knew Campion for a dependable witness, and said, 'Start talking. All I can get out of these people is something about the Conscience of America. I never knew we had one.'

Campion looked at the big men and the girl. The chief said, 'That's all right, talk. This is the F.B.I.'

Campion gulped. 'Do you get here fast!' he murmured admiringly, and then told his story.

When he'd finished the chief said, 'Now we've got to find out several things. One, who the so-called Conscience of America is — and I reckon that's something for the F.B.I. to get their teeth into. Two, what is the meaning of this film you saw. Three, where is the corpse, if there is a corpse.'

Big Lief Sorensen said, 'Finding your corpse is the most important thing, I reckon, chief. Without a corpse you can't do a thing. But there's another thing you should do — grab that film!'

Patrolman Luke Campion said, 'Someone grabbed it before you, sir. It was removed from the projector.'

The chief looked at the Feds and said, gruffly, 'Looks like I got my hands full. Escaped convicts, lynchings and the Conscience of America all facing me. Reckon the F.B.I. had better cooperate right from the start, eh?'

Sorensen turned to his gangling companion. 'You know as much as I do, Pav. Get through to the office and ask for more men to be sent down. I need a lot for tomorrow morning, apart from what the chief requires. Oh, and see if we know anything about this Conscience of America.'

He was briskly efficient now, and it encompassed the quiet girl at his side. He smiled at her. 'You'd better get home, Bronya. But I'd like you to keep in contact with me — I shall want you to identify the men when we pick them up.'

Not 'if we pick them up', the girl noticed. She smiled but looked away quickly, said, 'Goodnight,' rather uncertainly and went away into the crowd. Sorensen quickly explained to the chief who she was. The chief said he knew her father, a good, decent man in a fair way of business.

Then the chief asked, 'Now, what do we do first?'

Without hesitation Sorensen said, 'I want a plain-clothes man posted in every shoe shop in town the moment they open tomorrow morning.'

The chief gulped. He said, vaguely, 'Sure, sure. But maybe you'll tell me why?'

'The trail I'm following has brought me here to Warren Bridge,' Sorensen explained slowly. They were moving across to the chief's car, so as to avoid the relief workers who were now all over the grass with their unfortunate patients.

'Maybe it links up with that other clue — that the second pair of escaping convicts were also heading for Warren Bridge. Okay. Now my guess is they'll lie low here, probably with friends, until the heat goes off. You'll have all roads watched, I guess?' The chief nodded emphatically. 'That means it'll be risky for 'em to try and leave this town. So, if they've got friends here, they won't try it.'

The chief said, 'What's that got to do with shoe shops?'

'We know that two men, probably the murderers of a farmer and his wife, exchanged clothes, with a couple of motorists. They didn't fit very well, I guess, but they'd do for a while. But they didn't take the shoes of those motorists, though they had a look at them. Most clothes fit at a pinch, but shoes are different.

'Now, what's the first thing our friends will do? They'll try to get shoes, yes? Because heavy prison boots will attract attention along with smart town clothes. Most likely they'll send a friend along to buy shoes the size they want. So I want your men to watch out for anyone asking for several pairs of men's shoes and not trying them on himself — or it might be a woman who comes, of course. It's unusual for anyone to buy shoes like that, so there should be no trouble in spotting the customer.'

The chief said, 'You'll have your men, G-man. And let me say I think that's mighty smart reasoning.'

They waited until the square had quieted, and the crowd was dispersing, and then they drove back to the police H.Q. Then, for the next three hours they sat in a room that grew foul with cigarette smoke, and collated all information as it came through.

Almost at once they identified their victim. Someone said that even without his teeth and glasses they were sure it was Charlie Konkonscwi, and the man who came up with the information added, as an afterthought, 'The Commie buzzard.'

They got hold of a tired Luke Campion

and asked him a question. He thought back. 'Sure, I know old Charlie,' he said. 'Old Mouthy, they've got to callin' him lately. I wouldn't be sure, but I guess it could be him.'

Ben Arcota, briskly efficient in a manner that made his Pavlova nickname seem inappropriate, rounded on the chief. He was taking notes for transmission to the F.B.I. field office.

'Chief, let's have all you know on Konkonscwi.'

The chief came out pat with the answers. 'He's well-known to us. We've run him in a few times for things like causing crowds to gather, for disturbing the peace by holding meetings when he shouldn't, and so on.' Then the chief showed he was a very fair man. 'He's not very popular here just now, because he goes round supporting Russia. There are people who say he's an agitator paid by Moscow, but we have no evidence of that.'

Sorensen said, 'How does he live?'

'He's an old man, a retired school teacher who lives on his pension. My opinion is he is — was? — a silly old man who liked to say things and cause a commotion. Looks like he went too far and antagonised some of our law-abiding citizens.'

Sorensen said, 'If he's been killed by a mob, it doesn't matter what politics Konkonscwi had, our job's to see that justice is done.'

The chief nodded, though he didn't seem to be over-bothered by the demise of Charlie Konkonscwi, Old Mouthy and troublemaker. Maybe old Charlie had been a pain in the neck to the chief for a very long time.

Then a call came in from the F.B.I. records department. Nobody had ever heard of an organisation called the Conscience of America.

'So,' said Sorensen, 'that's some information we'll have to dig up for ourselves.'

He was called back to the phone immediately. For some reason Ben Arcota — Pavlova — lifted his head and watched him, as if suspecting the identity of the late caller.

It was Bronya Karkoff. She was nervous, uncertain, spoke with confusion.

'Mr. Sorensen? I — I'm sorry, but I won't be around tomorrow. I don't feel so good, so I'm going to an aunt in Norfolk.'

Sorensen looked at the phone for a few seconds and thought that one out. Then he said, 'You will not go to Norfolk tomorrow, and you'll be available when I want you. You are the only person positively able to identify two men believed to have murdered a farmer and his wife and gone off in their car. I need you, and I'll have you arrested if you try to leave town. When I see you tomorrow I'll add to that reason.' Then his voice changed, it became humorous, less official-sounding. 'Now, be a good girl and go up to bed. And stop tormenting yourself with thoughts of dignity lost in the back of a car.'

Bronya said, 'Oh!' quickly, as if indignant and shocked, and immediately rang off.

Ben Arcota, he who was named Pavlova, said sourly, 'What have you got that I haven't?' Then saw his own remarkably plain face in a mirror and decided to evade the question.

Sorensen good-humouredly said, 'It's Bronya. She's feeling ashamed of herself for getting weak and sentimental in the back of the car.'

Arcota said, 'Sure, I know.' Mimicked, 'Please be my daddy, Lief.'

His superior said, coldly, 'You were listening?'

'I never missed a thing!' Arcota said, toughly, 'You're doin' fine with the girl, but watch or I'll cut you out, buddy. She's a heck of a nice piece of homework.'

Sorensen said, 'So she is, and I saw her first.'

And then a man was shown in to see them. A big, red-faced man in a fury of temper. A man who swung his legs in a curious manner, as though they were unusually heavy.

Frank Descoign.

# 8

## Unholy bargain

Arnold Whitwam saw a movement of the heavy curtain across the long, riverside windows, and abruptly ceased to drink. Panic thoughts chased each other through his mind the way they had been doing these last two or three days, and the whisky he drank didn't seem to help dissipate them.

He fought back against the swift-uprising fear that clamoured into a brain that was just a bit fuddled; he tried to tell himself that it was just wind.

But it wasn't. And a moment later knew for certain.

For a hand came into view, to grasp the curtain preparatory to parting it.

It was a lean, blue-veined hand, that could have belonged to an old man. And sight of it brought Whitwam stiff in his easy chair, the hair on his scalp rising, icy spasms cascading down his spine. The clamorous fear was back and riding riot in his veins, and a dry mouth croaked an exclamation that sounded so like — 'Konkonscwi!'

It was the drink he'd had that made him startle like that and mouth such an illogical thought. Because Konkonscwi was dead, and Arnold Whitwam had been there to watch him burn.

Many times since Arthur Whitwam had wished that he hadn't gone with the boys that afternoon. It had sounded so good, teaching the blasted Commies an example — something to make them think before opening their yapping mouths.

And the excitement of that ride out, the contagious hysteria that develops when a crowd collects — especially a crowd with drink inside them — had made it seem a savagely hilarious thing to do, to burn Old Mouthy who had talked so long about distributing the wealth and inciting disaffection among their employees . . . a man dangerous to their private interests.

But it had been a sobering ride home, and an uneasy time since. For a man cannot stay with a crowd all the time; there must be moments when he is alone, and then fear comes crowding in, and a small voice says, 'God, why'n Hades did you do it? It's all right Frank and the others saying no one will ever know who did it; what if someone does get to know?'

The curtain came back. The man wasn't Konkoncwi. He was as tall, though, and pretty near as lean. He wore a smart hat that seemed too small for him, and a suit that looked expensive but was short and baggy on him. He carried an automatic in his hand. Behind him was a younger, heavier, more brutish face . . .

But for one second Arnold Whitwam knew only relief because the dead hadn't risen.

They came into the room. The first man's face was more clearly revealed. Somehow it was the kind of face you couldn't ever remember; it was like all other faces you had ever seen . . . vague, sallow, thin. Just a face. Only the eyes might have been green, and just now they looked evil.

The eyes fixed on the bottle. A hand

came out and lifted it from the table, tilted it to a thin mouth and drank. The green eyes never left Whitwam, the gun pointed at his guts all the time.

Whitwam wetted his lips and framed the inevitable question. But the lean man spoke first. He handed the bottle to his companion, who drank, and he said, gratingly, 'We came from your brother.' At that Whitwam thought he knew them.

He put his glass down heavily and exclaimed, 'My God, you're from Halifax. You busted outa jail. Guestler and — and — ' He couldn't think of the other name.

Egghead said, 'Sure, sure.' What did it matter what names Whitwam ascribed to them? He crossed over and pushed the watchful Whitwam back into his chair. 'We wanna talk to you — siddown,' he said. Whitwam looked at the gun and sat.

Egghead said, 'We're on the run an' we want to hide up some place. I guess this place looks good to us — no one'll think of looking for us here.'

Whitwam got back some of his courage and exploded, 'My God, you're not staying here. What the hell do you think I am?'

Johnny came forward then and told him. Johnny hadn't paid much attention to his cellmate's rambling but in a matter of years you find you can pick up a lot of interesting information, all the same.

He growled, 'You're a crook, like your brother, only he got caught and put in the can. They couldn't nail you, so your brother kept his mouth shut. You were company promoters but you did something with some old women who didn't know what they were signing. The money went into building up the biggest canning factory in this district. Now you know what sort of a guy you are.'

Whitwam blustered. A lot of people had said much the same about him before, and he had been quick to bring his lawyer in to help him. But now he didn't have a lawyer handy, and that gun was disconcerting.

Johnny cut through the bluster: 'Your brother thinks you're double-crossing him. You said for him to take his rap and you would get lawyers to fight his case and try an' spring him outa jail because he was an old man. Old Rocky — '

'Rocky?'

'Rockefeller Whitwam is how he's known to us in Halifax jail. Old Rocky opines as how you don't want him outa jail, 'cause while he's there you handle the million yourself.'

Whitwam snarled, 'What million are you talking about?'

Egghead came in at that. Egghead was morose, bad-tempered. He didn't like a lot of talking. He snarled in turn. 'The million old Rocky says you got stashed away from them old women.'

Whitwam came to his feet, his face incredulous. 'The hell, there never was no million! It's the fool talk of a senile old man you've been listening to.'

Egghead, watching him, said, thinly, 'Well, a part of a million could do for us now. We won't argue about a coupla zeros.'

Whitwam shouted, 'You won't argue about anything. I'm not gonna have a coupla convicts hidin' up in my house. Get to hell outa here!'

Egghead lost patience and hit him. It was a hard blow, delivered with a bony fist that split the cannery-owner's lips wide open and sat him down on the thick pile carpet.

Johnny shoved his gun out of sight and came across. He was snarling. Nothing had gone right since their breakout from jail. He felt like hitting somebody. Egghead picked Whitwam up. Johnny knocked him about the face. Then Egghead dropped him and started kicking into him. There was no purpose to it; they didn't know what gain would come from it. But it felt good.

Whitwam kept trying to shout, but the boys knew what they were doing. Every time he opened his mouth they hit him in the face or kicked him in the stomach.

They were just getting down to it when Egghead paused and lifted up his bald cranium to listen. Outside a car was drawing up . . . and another . . . and another. A lot of cars. Perhaps a dozen or so. Probably some had come seconds earlier without being heard, for even as Egghead turned to look at the curtained window, a man came striding through — a man with curiously heavy limbs, and a big, rough, red face.

He was so excited that he didn't seem to notice the curiousness of the situation — that the man he wanted should be bleeding about the face at the feet of two curiously dressed men.

He was shouting, 'For Pete's sake, Arnold, you don't know what's happened! They've got my place watched, an' Heppy's, Gowiddis' an' nearly everybody's. So we thought we'd all meet here — '

Now he saw that something was wrong; perhaps for the first time saw a couple of guns levelled at him. He came back to earth abruptly, said, 'What the hell! Who're these guys, Arnold?'

Whitwam climbed painfully to his feet and went across to a chair doubled up. He said, most curiously, 'Just a coupla friends who called.' Perhaps the gun, pointing his way, brought out that inappropriate word.

But things were happening. The room was getting crowded. Uneasy, nervous men were pouring in through that open window, not knowing what was going on inside that room. Frank Descoign leaned his weight against the press, but they just kept shoving him forward.

Egghead shouted, 'Stand back or you'll get yours!' But it was useless, against that uncomprehending tide. Ten seconds later everybody was standing close up against everybody else, and as a means of threat or of escape those guns were valueless. And the escaped prisoners knew it.

Someone knocked the gun out of Egghead's uncertain grasp; a hand quickly plucked the automatic from Johnny's fingers. Then Frank Descoign lifted his bull voice to get everybody back against the walls. 'Let's see what's going on,' he kept shouting.

They pushed back, leaving a small, clear space in the centre of the room.

Frank eyed the convict keenly and said, 'We wanna talk Arnold. Who're these guys?'

For some reason known only to himself, Arnold Whitwam lifted a mouth that was bleeding on to a big white handkerchief and said yet again, 'Oh, a coupla friends, I guess.'

So Frank said, 'Friends? Yeah, yeah, friends. Well maybe your friends wouldn't mind steppin' into another room while we talk over some important business, Arnold.'

Someone opened a door and Egghead and Johnny went across to it. Arnold Whitwam spoke from his chair 'Maybe someone oughta keep a gun pointin' at 'em while they're in there.'

Big Frank Descoign said again, vaguely, 'A gun? Sure, some of the boys'll oblige.' And half a dozen went out to mount guard, and no one thought it a curious way to treat friends.

Johnny Delcros glowered and then exploded, 'For Pete's sake, this is one heck of a town!'

First that cop car. It had shoved them into the side of the street, then a cop had come across and looked in on them. They'd had their guns ready, but out of sight. But all the cop had said was, 'It's against local ordinance to use headlights within the city limits. If this weren't a courtesy week you'd get a ticket. As it is

134

— *keep those goddam lights off, can't you?*' and with that the courtesy cop had stamped away.

And now a whole bunch of screwballs had risen up out of the ground and made them prisoner, and yet again nobody seemed to want to identify them as convicts on the run

Egghead mused 'Those guys sure got somep'n on their minds,' and watched for a momentary distraction that would enable him to spring across and grab his gun back.

In the next room a lot of men with a whole lot on their minds were bringing Arnold Whitwam up to date with things. And as he listened a pallor came to his face and the ache of his bruises was forgotten.

Big Frank Descoign threw another rage and shouted an explanation, 'Some nosey guy went up with a camera an' took a movie of Old Mouthy goin' out. It got us all in the film. You too, Arnold. Then tonight a bunch callin' themselves the Conscience of America went and screened that film publicly in the Southern Star

— *my movie house!* Mine!' That thought made him blasphemous.

It took minutes for the significance of all this to sink into Arnold Whitwam's mind, and it wasn't helped by the way the other men got to shouting at him to try to explain things quickly. Everybody was jumpy, nervy, with a feeling of urgency, yet not knowing what to do about it.

So Stef Gowiddis, who cleaned most things for Warren Bridge citizens, shouted for some order. For a gathering of leading citizens, this meeting was a most disorderly affair. He was an incisive man, Gowiddis, able to see a point and explain it clearly. They gave him a hearing.

'You won't get anywhere, behaving like this.' He was bitingly sarcastic, and all at once the excitement drained from them and left them quiet and ashamed and ready to listen. 'Don't you realize, we're in a hell of a mess, and it's times like these that we should keep our heads?'

He shoved his glasses up against his eyes in a characteristic gesture, and surveyed his audience before continuing. 'Don't you see what's got to be done

— quickly? There's that body — it's got to be taken and hidden away, that is if the police haven't already found it. And then there's that film. That's evidence sufficient to give some of us the gas chamber and others life.' He saw faces go suddenly pinched about the nostrils as fear gripped them.

Frank Descoign butted in then. He had a habit of butting in when other people seemed to be taking the lead; for Frank Descoign couldn't stand being second to anyone, couldn't stand being ordered around at all.

Descoign shouted, because that was his natural way of speaking: 'Doggone it, Stef's right on the nail. Without that corpse and film there's not a thing can be done to us. We gotta go collect that body right now.'

It had been a contemptuous gesture to leave Old Mouthy's body up there in the lonely glade. They had felt arrogantly safe; for without witnesses how could the killing be pinned to them, even if the body were ever identified? And they had felt particularly safe; because of the numbers who had been complicit in the crime.

But now, because someone had filmed the burning of Konkonscwi that corpse if found by the police could be the most damning evidence against them.

Everyone started saying, 'Sure, we gotta get that corpse hid away, an' we gotta find the buzzards with that film,' and then everyone went silent and didn't look at each other.

Frank Descoign said, 'What the hell?' then understood, and suddenly, for all his guts, he shared their feelings.

Gowiddis came in with a sneer. 'It's your stomach's keepin' you quiet, huh? There's none of you want to go and handle that corpse, huh?'

Someone from the back of that crowded, smoke-filled lounge said, uncertainly, 'It kinda sticks to your hands, burnt flesh. And it don't smell nice. Me, I couldn't do it, I know I couldn't.'

There was a general growl from everyone present. Gowiddis said, 'Well, someone's got to do it.' And then someone else raised a good point.

Old Hepburn said, 'I guess by now the police know most of us who were on that film. Looks like it because they're out waiting for us when we go home, we've been told. Okay, how're we gonna play detectives an' get aholt o' that film? I wouldn't know where to begin, and besides we got so much work to do I don't see how I could give the time.'

Five minutes later Arnold Whitwam began to see a way of ridding himself of a lot of embarrassments and he spoke up.

'Them two guys next door,' he began, when they'd hushed to listen to him. 'Look, maybe they could do all this work for us.'

Descoign's eyes were big and round and hard as he said, 'You say they're friends of yours?'

Whitwam came out with the truth now. It didn't seem to matter at all compared with the major threat that had developed.

'They're from Halifax jail. They got away today — didn't you see it in the papers? That fool brother of mine told them to come to me, and now they're looking to me to hide them, God knows why.'

Descoign said, 'Why did you say they were friends?' because he trusted nobody.

'I didn't like to have 'em talking about my brother in, front of you.' Whitwam had found some bottles and now he started to pour himself a drink with a hand that shook a little. 'I mean, would you want to start talking about a brother doing time in jail if you could help it? I know you all know he's there, but it's so long since it happened nobody ever speaks of it now.'

Descoign said, 'What's your idea?'

Whitwam pulled out a cheque book. 'I'll pay a thousand dollars into a pool. If you all do that — even the comparative few here — it adds up to a fortune. It totals so big, those boys next door would do anything to get their hands around it — even handling burnt corpses, I reckon. Maybe *even bumping off a few guys to get hold of that film for us!*'

Someone said, 'Just you hold on about this bumpin' off talk. We got ourselves in deep enough already.'

Descoign snapped, 'Whitty didn't say there would be bumping off. But, hell if it came to the point wouldn't we all bump someone off if it saved our skins? For crissake face up to it — we're in a jake so much we might have to do a whole lot more to get ourselves in the clear.'

There was an uneasy silence after that. Then someone else said, wearily, 'Looks like we got ourselves on to a wheel an' we can't get off the blamed thing. Whether we want to or not, I guess we just gotta go round where it takes us.'

They fetched Egghead Schiller and Johnny Delcros into the room. Big Frank Descoign took it upon himself to make the proposition. He was to the point about it.

He said, 'It was a long shot, thinking you'd be safe here with Arnold Whitwam. Only it didn't come off, did it?' Neither Johnny nor his hairless companion spoke; both stood hunched, waiting suspiciously for what was to come. Descoign continued: 'If we like we can get the police in at you.'

Johnny Delcros snarled, 'The hell,

Whitwam wouldn't dare. We know too much about him from his brother. He told us a lot, Whitwam.'

Arnold Whitwam let a sigh trickle through his cracked lips. 'Sure, I can guess what my brother had to say. He started sayin' things at the trial, but nothing could be pinned to me because I hadn't done anythin' wrong.' The way he said it, nobody was quite convinced, but politely everyone let it by without comment.

So Witwam said, dispassionately, 'You were too ready to believe. But I've got nothing to fear, and it wouldn't worry me none to have to hand you over to the police. Guess I could live down the talk it'd start again about my erring brother.'

So Egghead snarled, 'Then give us this proposition you're gonna cook up.' He wasn't so dumb at times, and it was obvious that something was cooking up.

Descoign said, 'We'll help you escape and we'll set you up for life, if you'll do a few things for us.'

'Such as?'

'Remove a burnt corpse and find some

guys and part them from a can of film we don't want them to have.'

Egghead was suddenly at ease. It was a proposition both he and Johnny could appreciate. Johnny went across and helped himself to a drink and then came in to do some bargaining.

'And what do we get out of it?'

'I'm not sure, but it should be well over thirty thousand dollars. Depends how many can afford the stake.' Johnny didn't fully understand, but his eyes, narrowed by early years of slugging around the fight ring, took on a cunning look. He said, 'Okay, give us the money and tell us where to find the stiff — '

'Hold on,' said Descoign. When it came to bargaining these convicts were up against experts. 'You won't get a cent until you come to us with that can of film.'

Egghead started snarling bad-temperedly. Frank Descoign told him brutally, 'The hell, d'you think we're mugs to trust you? Look, we'll provide you with a safe place to hide for as long as this job lasts, we'll fix you with disguises that you can travel anywhere without trouble, and when you've got that stiff outa the way and you've brought the film to us, we'll give you thirty grand plus.'

Egghead said, suspiciously, 'How do we know you'll keep your side of the bargain?'

Big Frank Descoign told him the truth. 'We've just got to do. It won't be in our interests to let the police capture you in case you open your mouths and talk. We'll complete our side of the contract, don't you worry.'

Egghead let his green eyes trail across to meet Johnny's. There was satisfaction in them. Johnny nodded. Egghead said, 'Okay, we're on. What do we do first?'

Descoign looked them over critically. 'We'll fix you with a wig, brother, and you'll both need to grow moustaches. And then we'll go out and get clothes for you that won't attract attention like these do. And shoes to match.'

\* \* \*

Three minutes earlier Joe Guestler had suddenly abandoned all the flimsy plans he had previously made. He was on to something much better now — so much better he was willing to overlook such a little thing as a double-cross.

# 9

## The Conscience of America

It was in every paper in America next day. At first abbreviated accounts of the Warren Bridge tragedy only appeared, but later editions carried fuller stories, and then the Press began to divide in its views on the situation, as the press always does.

Curiously the fate of the victims in the Southern Cross didn't seem to rank high in the editorial opinions. The glamour, if the word can be used, was all centred around the burning of the old ex-teacher in that glade among the oaks.

The liberal and moderate Press deplored that in a land of justice men should take it unto themselves to behave so barbarously, as well as illegally. And they cried out that the lynch-mob should be brought to trial and made to atone for their brutality.

But there was another, probably even stronger section of the Press that shouted a different opinion.

This was America, the land of free men. Frank Descoign and the citizens who had lynched the preacher of a totalitarian and alien philosophy were patriots. There were decent people who would no longer tolerate subversive activity in their midst, permitted by a lax and too-liberal constitution.

In a matter of hours the Warren Bridge lynching had become a major issue throughout the States, and occupied the premier position in any paper in the land.

Warren Bridge was on the map. By midday the place was crowded with reporters and photographers, and then came representatives of various societies and organisations, some to do what they could to secure indictment of the lynchers, others to assure the Descoign party that they had strong support for their actions. A deputation even visited the movie-proprietor in an effort to get him to say something that would precipitate a trial even without that film or before the corpse had been found.

But when they had gone, big, heavy

Frank Descoign just looked at some of his friends who had dropped in and said, grimly: 'It's my neck they're talkin' about. The hell, I'm sayin' nothin'. And I only hope that they find that Konkonscwi carcase an' bury it away so's no one'll ever find it. Then I'll sleep easier.'

Geordie Humble said the convicts had gone off at dawn — they'd gone out in a truck driven by Tom Dryway. The police weren't likely to stop him and search his truck: so that should be safe enough.

Descoign growled, 'There ain't nobody safe, not until we get rid of the blamed corpse an' destroy that film. That's why I risked things last night and went to see the police chief. Don't think I wanted to go!'

'But it turned out safe enough?'

'Sure, sure.' Descoign nodded viciously. 'I went as a man full of indignation because of what had been done in a movie-theatre owned by my company, and because of what was being said about me. They grilled me, but I denied everything and kept shouting I'd get a lawyer. When they let me go I knew what

I'd gone there to find out — they hadn't come across Konkonscwi, neither had they the film. So that gives me time in which to work, fellars, but — we gotta move fast. The Feds were already there when I reached the chief's office.'

Humble said, uneasily, 'It's uncanny, the way they pop up. They seem to smell things out . . . '

★ ★ ★

Up in Washington a man opened a newspaper and at once ceased to pulp the end of a cigar with fat wet lips And when he had finished he said, 'The double-crossin' two-timin' so and so, I hope his guts drop out!'

Then he got through to Hymie Kolfinkle and asked a question. Hymie lied the first three times, then came up with the truth when his boss's disbelief became too brutally expressed. He said, weakly, 'Yeah, Reimer asked me so I told him. I should have known, he asked me so nicely, not like his usual way of talkin'. He said, 'Hymie, where from did you get

149

them pictures?' So I told him. But what does that matter? Or does it?'

The boss said, 'Maybe it does. The papers say the cops are tryin' to locate the corpse. Only you knew where it was, Kolfinkle. Now that buzzard Reimer knows, and maybe by now a whole lot more people also know. You don't know Reimer?'

Kolfinkle said, 'No.'

The boss spoke viciously, bitterly. 'He's a born troublemaker, that guy. Whatever it is, he's agen it. He was agen the war with Japan an' Germany, him an' a lotta friends, an' he got a jail sentence which didn't turn him any friendlier. He knows the Conscience of America.'

He was about to switch off when he remembered something

'About that rise, Kolfinkle.'

Hymie said, 'Yes?' quickly.

The boss said, 'You can forget it.'

Hymie put down the phone feeling more than usually depressed, for last night, to get some relief from his wife, he had told her of the bigger pay cheques to come.

But if he was depressed his boss was

much more so. Because it now seemed imperative that he went to the police and told them what he knew.

Well, he would tell them something, anyway.

★   ★   ★

Next morning, even before Warren Bridge was astir, information started coming in about the Southern Star episode. The first published reports about the Conscience of America produced results.

Lief Sorensen, tired but not showing it, was there to collate the information. Washington F.B.I. came through. He heard a Records man ask, 'You were wanting information about an organisation called 'The Conscience of America'?'

Sorensen said. 'Yes,' so quickly, so eagerly, that the straw thatch of his assistant jerked up from out of a doze at the sound of it.

'It's a crackpot affair with members living mostly in Virginia, the Carolinas and Georgia,' Records said. 'They're an anti-lynching outfit. Whenever there's a lynching they go and raise hell here in Washington. They have always been law-abiding, and for that reason we have no record of them.'

Sorensen said, 'Who's at the head? We want the bird because he holds vital evidence in this Southern Cross tragedy.'

Records came up pat with all the information. 'Alabaster Morgan is head of the show; lives in New Bern, N.C.'

Sorensen said, 'Is that his real name?' Record confirmed it was. Sorensen said, 'With a name like that you can't blame the guy for going around digging up trouble . . . Put a call through to the New Bern field office for them to pick up Alabaster Morgan and his associates.'

Half an hour later, with the warm sun just rising, Records came through with an amendment.

'We've just discovered that Alabaster Morgan isn't the big white chief any more. Seems he got deposed recently for not pursuing a more aggressive policy. A new bunch have taken over, and they don't seem as nice as Morgan. The new chief is a crackpot with a police record for violence. He's called Calvin Brodhunk, and he gets mixed up with all sorts of extremist movements, only he's the guy that makes 'em extreme.'

Sorensen said, 'Put out a general call for Calvin Brodhunk. I've an idea he might be getting into more mischief.'

He was. The chief came in after a few hours' sleep just as a call came through from Signals Branch. Sorensen took the message.

'A call just came in from Patrol Car V5. They report they can see a column of fire like from gasoline in the Crombie foothills. The patrol car's heading up there right away. *They say they looked through glasses and it seemed like a fellar was burning in the middle of that fire.*'

Sorensen rapped, 'Tell that car to keep in close touch with H.Q. and to report all their findings to me immediately.'

He turned and told the chief what had been seen. The chief said, 'For a small town we sure do see life, don't we?' Then the bell was ringing, and again it was Washington on the line for Sorensen.

'A fellar's just been in. He's boss of a corporation that takes news-films. He says he knows all about that film that caused the bother; says he saw it a few days ago but thought there was some hocus about it so he just left it lyin' around and someone must have walked off with it. That's his story, anyway. He says his film editor, a mischief-maker with a record called G. Rudolf Reimer, hasn't shown up today, so he reckons he's the fellar that walked off with the film.'

Sorensen said, 'Who took the film, and where was it shot?' Because they had to get hold of that body before anyone else got around to it.

Washington said, 'An operator named Hyman Kolfinkle took the film. He's been interviewed and says it was some place off the road that leads from Warren Bridge out to the Crombie Range.'

Sorensen nodded with sudden satisfaction. 'I guess we're on to the place right now.'

Then Washington F.B.I. asked a question.

'How's the search for your convicts

going, and for the killers of that farmer and his wife?'

'Could be they're all the same,' returned Sorensen. 'We think they're hiding out here in Warren Bridge. We're following an idea that might lead us to them in the next few hours.'

Washington was affable. 'They've got nothing to do with the Southern Star business, I suppose?'

Sorensen was surprised. 'I wouldn't think so. It's just coincidence that a lot of things have happened around this town all at once. No, I guess they're not linked in anyway.'

Which proves even the F.B.I. cannot know everything.

Things continued to happen within the next hour. The radio car came through with a description of the scene within a glade of oaks. The place had taken a bit of finding.

They'd found the charred corpse of a man lying across a burnt gasoline can. All around was a blackened patch, as though gasoline had burned in a flaming pool, and the man had died within it. No, there was nothing they could see to identify the corpse.

Sorensen said, 'But do they think that this corpse has been burnt in the last hour or so, or could it be the corpse of the man burnt when the Southern Star film was taken, some time ago?'

The radio car came back to say. 'We couldn't tell. It'll need a doctor.'

Sorensen said, 'He's on his way. He was sent twenty minutes ago.' And then he sat back to await the next development.

It came just about the time that plain-clothes men were reporting to various shoe shops around the town. The chief was in with Sorensen again when it happened — Sorensen was directing the search, but the chief couldn't keep out of it. Sorensen liked the old boy and didn't mind his frequent bobbing-in for information,

Sorensen was pinpointing a position on a wall map when the next remarkable event occurred. The chief saw that it was in the foothills of the Crombie Range, where the burnt body had been found.

The door was opened by an incredulous cop, and six elderly men walked in. They were all thin men, stringy, with corded old necks and bleak white faces. They were pretty well-dressed, and most wore glasses. Just a bunch of guys, Sorensen was thinking, when one of the men cleared his throat and said, raspingly, 'We are the Conscience of America.'

Sorensen didn't show the shock he felt at the announcement. He crossed to his chair and sat down. The chief wheeled away from the wall map and stood, legs astraddle, with the morning sun warm as it came through the window at his back. He spoke first. He said, 'Maybe after last night you've got something on your conscience, too.'

The spokesman just ignored that remark. Watching him, Sorensen thought: The foxy old devil, he's thinking of ways out for himself!

The foxy old devil said, 'I'm Alabaster Morgan. I am a man of high conscience. For years I have declaimed against the devil in men's hearts, especially in the matter of lynching. To help me, I recruited men of like mind — ' His hand jerked in an embracement of the old men with him. 'But some of my followers were not without evil themselves, it seems, and in the last days I was deposed from leadership and became just a follower without influence to the movement.'

Sorensen thought: Brother, you're trying to evade responsibility for what happened last night. But people died in that stampede . . . He heard the chief sniff contemptuously.

Alabaster Morgan moaned piously, 'There was a man named Calvin Brodhunk, who claims descent from Lynch, the North Carolina farmer who long ago gave his name to punishment without trial by law. He believed in the Mosaic law — an eye for an eye. He said the way to stop lynching was to lynch the miscreants. I opposed the theory as long as I could.' He kept getting in phrases like that, over-emphasising them.

'But Brodhunk secured the support of some of our brethren. He it was who spoke at the Southern Cross last night — '

'But you were in approval of the showing of the film?' That was the chief, blunt and to the point.

Alabaster looked bleak, then had the bright idea of ignoring the interruption. He went on, while the thin old men drooped dejectedly about him, 'And it was Brodhunk's idea, what happened this morning.'

Sorensen said, 'Tell us what happened this morning.'

So Alabaster told them everything. Reimer had told Brodhunk where the film had been taken, how the body had been left in that lonely glade. Brodhunk was shrewd and had made a guess that after the showing of that sensational film the lynchers would at once go and dispose of the body — suddenly it would be too dangerous to be left for the police to find.

'We went to lie in wait for whoever came along. Oh, yes, we found the body there, lying where it had fallen beneath the scorched branches of a solitary oak tree. We hid, and then a truck drove up at dawn. There were three men in it; one sat behind the wheel while the other two came up with a sack in their hands.'

The Conscience of America had jumped out upon the men as they approached the corpse. Whereat the two men unexpectedly drew revolvers and told them to stand still if they wanted to go on living.

Alabaster Morgan licked his lips painfully. That, curiously, was something they hadn't expected — that two or three men should turn the tables on them so easily. They didn't carry firearms themselves, 'Until the last few days we were pledged to a policy of reform without violence,' Alabaster explained. And for some reason they hadn't thought that their quarry might carry weapons.

Sorensen asked, 'What did you intend to do with the men who came to collect that corpse?'

Alabaster said, 'They were to have trial, and then sentence.'

'And then you were going to burn them alive, just as they had burnt Konkonscwi, the agitator?'

Alabaster threw up his skinny hands in horror. Oh, no, that wasn't the idea. They were going to frighten the men, then leave them tied up against a tree until they were discovered by the police with that corpse right before them.

And then he admitted that there had been talk of effecting retribution in that manner. Brodhunk, the descendant of the first lyncher, had wanted to burn the men when they came, and he had talked wildly and with great passion and had secured some support for his idea. The way some of the old men looked uneasy made Sorensen think that they had been among Brodhunk's supporters.

But the old men's plans had gone all awry. Those guns were an unexpected factor in the situation.

One man covered the Conscience of America with a gun, while the other kicked the charred corpse into a sack and then carried it back to the truck. Alabaster Morgan said that there was so little corpse that the man carried it lightly in one hand.

Alabaster had to think what happened next; everything had happened so quickly.

He said that suddenly Brodhunk came

charging round a car with a gasoline can in his hand. He was shouting wild things, and the gasoline was splashing out of the open neck. Alabaster said that one of the men let fly with a stream of shots, and old Brodhunk went staggering down on to his knees and then fell on to the spilling can. The next minute there was an explosion and the gasoline roared up into a pillar of fire, with Brodhunk dead and burning in the middle of it.

They didn't know what had caused the gasoline to fire, but Alabaster thought it might have been a shot that did it, or a spark as the can hit a stone.

'But what did you do then?'

Apparently everybody just went into a flat spin and ran for their cars, including the gunmen. The Conscience of America fled, then later got together to discuss the situation.

'And then you gave yourselves up.' That was the chief, and he was rough with his tongue. In a gentle roar he said, 'You're a lot of dozy old crackpots. You've been the means of killing several nice people and hurting a lot more in that stampede last night. Now you think that by putting all the blame on to the dead Brodhunk you will be allowed to get away with your stupidity.' He breathed heavily, then turned to Sorensen. 'But they're your men, Sorensen. What do you want with them?'

Lief said, 'A description of the corpse-gatherers; after that they're yours.'

The chief said, 'Then the silly old donkeys'll sit in the cooler for a week or two, and that'll give 'em time to think on what they have done.'

Sorensen got the descriptions. They could have been anybody; the old boys were so inexact and contradictory. The men were being led away when old Alabaster Morgan turned and said, uneasily, 'There's something else. That film was in my car. I forgot to tell you that one of the men crossed over and got it before Brodhunk got around with his gasoline can.'

The Conscience of America could hear the chief's voice roaring after them when they were yards on their way down to the cells. In time he quieted, and then he said. 'What do we do now? No corpse, no film. That means no proof that there ever was a crime committed!'

Sorensen said, slowly, 'Get out and arrest Frank Descoign and other people named. We don't have the film, but we have the evidence of a lot of Southern Star patrons who saw it. And we also have a corpse — Brodhunk's, according to the Conscience of America. But why should we believe them? Why shouldn't it be Konkonscwi the Red?'

The chief stared, and then he started chuckling. And then he said, 'By God, that's good. The patrol car said there was nothing left to identify.' He slapped his thigh in sudden good humour. 'We got a corpse, right in the place where we were told to find it. That's good enough for me just now.'

And then that overworked telephone rang again.

Someone had bought two pairs of footwear for men bigger than himself.

# 10

Some men, one girl,
a can of film . . . and a corpse

The room was filling with big, intelligent-looking huskies, and the excitement seemed to mount so that the very air was alive with tension.

For Sorensen had grabbed the police chief and was trying to make him understand. Trying, though he was still working out the idea himself.

He said, 'Don't you see, it's not just a smart trick. The corpse of Konkonscwi and the film are vital evidence. Especially that film. If it is destroyed the lynch mob can sit back and laugh at any witnesses we might produce. Well, it looks like some members of the lynch mob have got hold of the film — and the body — and you can bet they'll destroy both just as soon as they can. All right, ask yourself, how soon can that be?'

The chief stared. The athletic young men stood around and waited. Even Sorensen was trying to work that one out for himself. 'Those men got the film less than an hour ago, according to those old crackpots cooling in the cells. Maybe they'll just go a mile or so, then hide both by burying them some place. But my guess is they won't.'

The chief asked a flat, 'Why?'

'Look,' said Sorensen. He'd got things taped now. 'They won't try to bury the charred corpse or that film, not within a hundred miles of the Crombie Range highway. Because they know that if need be we'll dig up every square yard of earth to find them. *They* know that. Okay. They'll try to perform a more thorough act of destruction on both, and that means taking them somewhere where it is safe to work on them.

'That's why I want every known member of that lynch mob to be brought in and jailed — because if we hold them in jail they can't be destroying things. And that's what I want you for.' Sorensen wheeled on the newly arrived bunch from the nearest F.B.I. field office. He rapped, 'The chief will make out the warrants; I want you to pick up all suspects of that lynch mob and clap 'em behind bars. You, chief, must resist all attempts to bail 'em out until we know how we stand in regard to that corpse and film.'

The chief said, 'It's a good plan, though it's full of holes. We don't know everyone connected with that lynching affair.'

But Ben Arcota came in to argue for Sorensen. He said, 'We know the ringleaders, the fellars whose skin is in danger. They're the people who did the actual burning. My guess is it's within that group we'll find the men responsible for routing the Conscience of America this morning.'

The chief said, 'I'm with you.' He went out of that office as though suddenly charged with atomic energy, and the G-men who were to run in the lynch mob streamed after him.

Ben Arcota said, 'That call that came in about someone buying shoes?'

Sorensen told him, 'The customer is being trailed. The detective shadowing him phoned back to say that he was also buying clothes for two men. He also told me his name.'

The way he paused Ben Arcota knew there was something puzzling him. He said, 'Finish it. Something's biting you raw.'

So Sorensen said, 'The fellow's a well-known industrialist. His name's George Humble. He's a director of Humble & Dryway, Inc., chemical manufacturers.' Then he leaned forward helplessly. 'What I can't get over is that we have his name down as a ringleader of this lynch mob.'

Ben Arcota's colourless features jerked up. 'You're not thinking that our convict friends might be mixed up in this lynching business?'

Sorensen walked away from the desk and brooded out of the window. Then he said, 'I don't see how it can be. Just a coincidence, I suppose, But remember what the Conscience of America said — those dozy old donkeys. They said that two gunmen with automatics held them up when they interfered over that corpse. I'm thinking that lynch mobs generally consist of fairly ordinary citizens, and ordinary citizens don't tote guns around like professional gunmen. And Alabaster Morgan gave the impression that they were professionals in the use of automatics.'

Ben Arcota kept looking at him, trying to absorb all the implications that his chief put over. 'My God,' he said, 'you're thinking that some of those escaped convicts, all of whom are professional gunmen, might be in on this lynching affair!'

Sorensen said, firmly, 'I'm thinking nothing of the sort. I'm just considering all the facts, and seeing where they lead. But I'm not going beyond them. We've two cases to crack while we're down here, and we seem to be doing the only thing possible to solve them.'

Then he told Ben to go fetch Bronya Karkoff. 'I think the time's come when we need her. I'm expecting a call through from the man who's tailing Humble, the chemical manufacturer. When Humble ends this shopping expedition we might know where the murderers of that farmer and his wife are hiding. Okay, Bronya's needed in case we have to identify the men. First charge will probably have to be one for robbing the filling station and assaulting Bronya.'

Ben Arcota went out saying. 'It's Bronya now, huh?' but Sorensen was unperturbed. He knew that Pavlova was only kidding in pretending to be jealous.

Ten minutes later came a call from the detective who'd been on Humble's trail. His voice was a wail of mortification. 'I got snagged up in some traffic down Bridgewater Street and I lost him. He went heading west, that's all I know.'

Sorensen put the receiver down with a crash. It had been a slender thread they had been following, but their only one. And now it had snapped.

And in this race against time they couldn't afford to waste minutes picking up a new trail.

Suddenly he went racing down towards the chief's room. He was crossing the head of the main stairway when he saw Bronya and Ben Arcota coming up. He paused, grabbed Bronya's hand long enough to pat it, and say. 'Good girl for coming,' then dived into the chief's room.

Ben said, gloomily, 'That's the sort of guy he is,' because she was looking bright-eyed at the sight of big Lief Sorensen.

Bronya said, 'I think he's nice.' And when Ben started to argue she shut him up by saying, innocently, 'You still haven't told me why they call you Pavlova.'

The chief looked up when Sorensen came banging in. He said, nodding sagely, 'Don't tell me, something's gone wrong!' and Lief nodded.

'We've lost the trail. Your man got held up and George Humble went west. We've no time to lose. I want to know all about Humble, anything that might tell us where he might be going out of town.'

A police captain swung round from a desk behind the chief's. The chief nodded. 'Go ahead, captain. You know George Humble better than I do. You tell him — quick.'

'Humble's a bad name for him,' said the captain. 'He's a belly-aching so-and-so. The fights we've had over one damn' thing and another . . . Anyway, he's in business with Tom Dryway. They make soap, dyes, tanners' solutions and other chemical products. They've got houses in the swank riverside area — '

Sorensen said, 'Humble wasn't going back there. He was heading west, last seen.'

'And the Humble & Dryway chemical factory isn't west either, it's down river,' said the captain. So then they all stared at each other until Lief Sorensen got up and said. 'This isn't getting us any place. Get to thinking again, captain. Humble is on his way westwards out of town; I've a suspicion he's going to where a couple of killers are in hiding. That means, from Humble's point of view, it must be some safe place — you wouldn't, in any event, call a busy factory or a man's private home safe, would you? So . . . what other places has Humble got?'

The captain was shaking his head slowly. So Sorensen tried again. 'Is he in any other kind of business?' But then the chief started snapping his fingers in excitement.

'You give me an idea, Sorensen.' He wheeled on the captain. 'Humble came into partnership with Dryway only a few years ago, and before that he had a small soap-making plant out on the Sand Lot, didn't he? And that place has been derelict and a damn' nuisance to everybody for a couple of years . . . '

Sorensen said, 'If that's west of Warren Bridge, it sounds the place.'

The chief picked up his hat. 'It is westwards, and I'm coming along with you. You F.B.I. men get all the fun. The hell, someone else can answer the phone.'

Three cars went out in convoy. The first contained Ben Arcota, driving, the chief, Bronya and Sorensen the other two bulged with hefty G-men, just returned with indignant, expostulating prisoners. The chief, directing the vehicle, said, 'It's queer that trails seem to be crossing. What I mean is, the only men on our lynch mob list that we haven't picked up are Tom Dryway and Geordie Humble. And now we are on their trail for quite another case.'

Ben looked into the eyes of his superior

through the driving mirror and said. 'Now someone else is trying to make one nice big case out of all this.'

So Sorensen said, 'Can you think of a better place in which to dispose of a partially burnt corpse than a chemical factory? And who'd be better men to employ to do the dirty work than a couple of killer convicts on the run?'

The chief said, 'Now fit Joe Guestler and Jud Corbeta into the picture and I'll die happy.'

They were running out on to the dreary Sand Lot now — a desolate wilderness of scrub growing precariously out of poor, stony soil. The chief told them that because of the smell Humble had had to build his first soap factory out here in the wastes, but it had been a bad choice of site because of the difficulty of getting labour to come so far out of town. Now it was derelict.

They rode on. Sorensen could feel that Bronya wasn't at ease beside him, and he didn't like it. With a girl as pretty as Bronya Karkoff a man likes to have everything in his favour.

So Sorensen thought things out in his own, patient, thorough way and he said, 'You're feeling somehow ashamed of yesterday still, aren't you? It seemed all right at the time but now your cheeks burn when you think of it. It now seems the corniest thing to do, doesn't it?'

She nodded, and her cheeks were red and burning. But he said it in such a way that it didn't seem quite so bad, after all.

He was laughing. 'Oh, come out of it, Bronya. You had a frightening time, and it made you behave just a little hysterically. Just forget it.'

She said, 'For a tough policeman, you're a charming man.'

And then he crowned it by leaning over her and saying, 'Anyway. I'd hate to be your daddy,' and there was no mistaking the meaning behind the words.

He settled back, saying rather loudly, 'And now I'll tell you the story of a G-man who takes ballet lessons in his spare time. The result of it all is that within the F.B.I. he is known as — '

'You're a heel,' said the driver nastily. 'You always do this with a girl because you're afraid of my competition.' His hair looked more like old straw than ever.

Then they stopped on the old stone track that wound between wind-eroded dunes. The chief said, 'We'll hide off the road. The factory is just over the hill. We've got to reconnoitre the place first, because we can't just go bustin' in on suspicion caused because a fellar buys a coupla pairs of shoes too big for himself.'

They bumped behind a rock screen and then piled out. The chief trudged up the soft, shifting sand, and the others followed. On top of the hill he sprawled face down and removed his hat before peering over the skyline. The others were equally as circumspect.

Below, set in the drab weed-grown, bush-infested wasteland, was the silent, tumbling factory. From this height they could look into it. They could see a long high factory with a falling, galvanized iron roof, a loading bay and an open yard or compound. There was a big wooden gate leading into the compound, but it was shut just now.

The chief pointed to the gates, saying,

'That seems to be the way in. The wall's too high to scale.'

Then Sorensen pointed and said, 'And there's someone inside, too.' He was pointing into a deep shadow thrown by the cover at the far end of the loading bay. He could just make out two vehicles standing there.

And one was a private car, and the other a truck.

Sorensen said, 'It could mean anything, that truck. Most firms have trucks, I reckon. But it answers the description of the vehicle the gunmen used when they met up with the Conscience of America.'

Then they all sat around and had a talk about things — Sorensen, for the first time, was feeling blue. He said, 'I guess we've arrived a bit late, if these are the boys we are after. If they've got the body of Konkonscwi and the film inside there, I reckon they'll have had time to destroy both. I can't see them hanging on to either, having gone to the trouble of collecting 'em.'

At that everybody felt blue, until the chief said, harshly, 'Harbouring criminals will be something to hold against Dryway and Humble, if the convicts are in there. Let's get 'em for that, anyway!' But the thrill had gone out of the chase, all the same. It felt bad, getting here just too late to secure that vital evidence . . .

Sorensen said, 'Okay, but what's the first move, chief? We're still working on surmise, and as you said, we've no evidence yet to permit us to go busting in there. And an even stronger argument, there might be some very desperate killers inside, men who won't hesitate to open up with guns.'

They went back to the cars to talk, so that the sound of their voices wouldn't carry over to the derelict factory. Bronya had come out of the car and was listening. Perhaps she wanted to acquit herself because of the weakness she had shown the previous day; for she suddenly said, 'I don't look like a policeman. I could go to the gates and knock and make some excuse like wanting to know how far it is to town. And if anyone came to the gate I could describe them to you later. *Don't forget that I know what two of them look like*!'

Sorensen said, 'And don't forget that two of them know what you look like, Bronya.'

Bronya gave thought to that and then said, 'They won't recognize me. I had a cap on and a greasy white monkey-suit. They won't know me.' She patted her hair confidently.

Sorensen thought that she did look a whole lot different — better.

The chief said, 'There's an idea in that. Maybe it would be better for this girl to make a closer reconnaissance for us. Just one thing. Stay outside on the roadway. Under no circumstances go inside that factory, understand?'

Bronya's eyes were bright. She nodded, then set off towards the road. Everyone else went ploughing back to the top of the dune. They saw her come out into the sun-bleached open and start to go across to the factory gates. Then Ben Arcota gripped Sorensen's arm and pointed silently far away over the top of the factory.

'A car,' whispered the G-man. 'I'll swear that wasn't there the last time we looked.' He called for some glasses — and trained them on it; found he could read the number plate, though the car was well-hidden among some bushes.

He slowly read out the registration number, and the chief went looking into his notebook.

'That,' he said, 'is a car that was reported stolen outside Warren Bridge late last night. Now, who could have used that?'

But no one was interested in the car now. Every eye was fixed on the girl who had been approaching the gate but had now suddenly stopped. Then they saw her start to move forward again; saw the gate open slightly. And the girl just walked in and disappeared from sight.

Startled, the chief rapped, 'What — ' And then froze.

For someone was lurking on the far side of the factory wall, was trying to force an entry by way of a little side gate. Had succeeded and got in. Two men. And now they were dropping a bar across the gate, so that no one else could get through the way they had come.

Then the yard was empty. Everyone must have gone inside that big rotting factory with its rusty, derelict machinery. Some men, one girl, a can of film . . . and a corpse.

# 11

## F.B.I. Showdown

When the truck came swinging into the old factory yard Egghead saw an automobile already parked far under the cover of the loading bay. He demanded, suspiciously, 'Who's car is that?'

Tom Dryway said, shortly, 'Mine. I came out in it to pick up this truck.' It was a lie and he expected them to say, 'You don't keep trucks out in a place like this,' but they didn't tumble to it and just got out with a lot of grunting.

Dryway opened up the old factory and walked inside leaving the convicts to come in with the body. He had tried to pick up the can of film casually, but Egghead had taken it rather quickly, saying, 'The hell, I c'n manage that.' So he hadn't pressed the matter. He held the whip hand, he and his friends.

No film — and corpse — no reward

and no assistance in keeping out of the hands of the police. That was the way he saw things at the moment. There was just one thing Tom Dryway had overlooked, and that came out later.

They went inside the factory. It looked bigger inside than without — rows of oil-fired, metal, rendering tanks, with crude steel agitators driven from overhead shafting, stretched as far as they could see. Steel gantries everywhere, forming floors of varying height, with steel steps leading up to them. And at one end even more massive, more intricate apparatus.

It was towards this end that Tom Dryway was leading them. They climbed some steps and came out on to a narrow metal gangway set alongside some big, steel-domed pressure vessels, now rusted red with disuse

Dryway started to unfasten the bolts attached to the heavy lid, and then turned for help to the two jail-breakers. They were just standing there, looking at him. The bulky sack was at Johnny Delcros's feet; Egghead had the can under his arm.

Dryway snapped, 'Come an' give a hand with this blasted bolt.' He was never a man for politeness, and just now he was in a boiling hurry to see the last of Konkonscwi the Red.

Egghead, leaner, paler, more formidable than his lowering, brutish companion, said thinly, 'We ain't in no hurry. Just now we could do with something to eat an' drink, I guess. You said there'd be food in the truck, but we ain't had time to stop an' eat yet.'

They turned to go back, leaving the sack on the floor, but Dryway saw that Egghead was still hanging on to the can of film. Dryway swore a lot but went on wrestling with the bolts. In time he got them off, and then tried to use the tackle to lift the lid, but it was rusty and he saw he'd need oil to get the wheels to move. He wiped his hands, looked at the sack, then hurried down after the convicts. He knew there'd be oil in the truck.

Egghead was standing close against the big gates when he came to the factory door. Johnny Delcros was in the shadow and reached out and grabbed him.

Dryway was startled and began to lash out, and then stood still as Johnny hissed, 'Blast you fer a fool, keep quiet, can't you! Something's gone wrong, somewhere!'

Dryway allowed himself to be pulled to a broken window that let out into the shadows of the loading bay. Then Johnny's growling voice said, 'It was Eggy. We was eatin' an' he got to lookin' around in the dust an' he saw footprints that led through that door we went in by. Funny, they must have bin there all along an' we never noticed 'em. For our tracks are on top of 'em.'

Dryway was looking at the footprints, and his heart was chilled. He said, 'You're sure they're none of ours?'

Johnny swore and said, savagely, 'The hell, you got eyes, ain't you? Them prints came from some small guy's feet wearin' cissy pointed shoes. An' we ain't got shoes yet. An' yours are much bigger.'

Dryway looked hard at the footprints, then slowly raised his eyes in time to receive another, far bigger shock.

Egghead was slowly swinging the gate

open. Someone was walking through.

It was a girl. Dark. Good-looking. Smartly dressed.

Then he saw that Egghead had a gun in his hand, was giving the girl orders. The girl and her captor came walking round to the bay, keeping close under the high wall all the way. Egghead kept looking round, his green eyes vicious. He snarled, 'There's a lot I don't like about this place. Get through that window, all of you.'

The girl started to protest, but Johnny pulled her through. She kept saying, 'I was just coming to ask the way to Warren Bridge — ' Then she shut up as Johnny said, 'I've seen your mug some place before. Now where sister, where?'

Egghead growled. 'Shut up, everyone.' His eyes were darting down the lines of rusting, collapsing plant. 'There's a guy still inside here, because he made only oneway footmarks. I want to know who he is and what he's doin' here.' And his mean eyes swung round to fasten on Dryway.

He snarled, 'This ain't no trap, I hope — ' His gun was fixed menacingly in line with Dryway's big stomach.

Dryway had guts. He swallowed and then said, 'Look, we came to an arrangement. We'll keep our part, but you gotta keep yours. That stuff's hot — you know what I mean . . . ' His eyes looked significantly towards Bronya. 'Help me fix it in a sulphonator with some waste sulphuric acid and you can collect your reward.'

Egghead was red-raw with suspicion of a double-cross and he went out snarling like a baited cat. 'Sure, like hell we will. An' what happens when the stuff's inside that thing and rotting in the acid? You'll say, 'The hell with thirty grand; that job wasn't worth it. Here's a coupla bucks, now beat it else we'll call a cop'. I wasn't born yesterday, smart guy!'

Johnny was catching on. He hadn't been thinking so far ahead. He said, admiringly, 'Eggy don't need to grow hair; he gets by with brain.' His own gun was pointing more at the sweating chemical product manufacturer than at the girl now, and Bronya wasn't missing a thing.

Egghead said a bit more. 'We're gonna sit around an' wait till your partner gets out with the dough and the clothing you promised us. When that's here I'll do a swap. Until then I'm holdin' on to this can of film.'

Unexpectedly a heavy voice said, 'That's what you think.' Then the voice said, as they were turning, 'Drop your guns without another move or you'll get drilled right through the back, the pair of you.'

Bronya looked past the convicts and saw a small, plump man close against the side of a big metal tank. He looked very natty, a typical small-town businessman, Only, unusual for a businessman, there was a serviceable-looking Colt in his hand.

And Bronya also decided that she'd seen more affectionate eyes in a snake than were back of this fellow's rimless glasses.

He spoke like a man who was used to giving orders and when they heard his tough, rasping voice both convicts knew that he wasn't bluffing. They froze, irresolute.

Dryway seemed to relax, hearing that voice. He stepped forward, saying, 'I knew you were somewhere around, Geordie, but I thought you were never going to show up!'

Dryway took the guns from the convicts, and then they were permitted to turn. They glowered at the plump little man with the hard eyes. He said, 'You palookas, do you think we'd trust men with your reputation? The hell, how d'you think we've got on in business? I came on ahead to make sure you didn't get up to any tricks when you arrived with the — er, stuff. You know what would have happened if I'd been here with the thirty grand? Sure as fate you'd have said it wasn't enough and you'd have started in to blackmail for more.'

The way Johnny and Egghead exchanged quick glances suggested that the plump little man hadn't been far off the mark.

But Egghead got worked up and snarled, 'You dirty little cheat, I'll stew you in your own pot for this.'

The little man — Bronya guessed he'd be George Humble, Dryway's partner

— jumped forward aggressively. He shouted, 'Call me names like that, you jailbird, and I'll save the State a job.' He motioned impatiently. 'For Pete's sake, let's get moving, I had a tail after me in town.'

That startled them.

Humble went on, 'We've got to get that stuff into an acid bath. Tom, get down and start some oil burning under one of the sulphonators. You two eggs, get the lid off it and start pouring in waste acid from the carboys you'll find outside.'

Even then Egghead tried to bargain. He growled, 'An' ef we do this? You said there'd be thirty grand in it for us.'

Geordie Humble, the tightest bargainer in Warren Bridge, looked coldly over the top of his glasses and said, 'You were prepared to break your part of the bargain. Okay, that lets us out of our side of the contract. Thanks for collecting Old Mouthy and that can.'

He was looking at Bronya and she didn't like the way he stared at her. He said, 'When this is over I'll be wanting to know how you came in on this scene

— and how vou're gonna leave.' Something in the way he said it chilled her. There was ominous threat in the words.

Tom Dryway went clambering out of sight under a staging, while small, firm Geordie Humble drove his prisoners before him. He showed them an old carboy carrier down one end of the shed and a lot of straw-protected carboys of waste acid, He ordered, 'Get 'em along and up to the staging.'

They got a dozen up, though they were sweating heavily by the time they had finished. And by this time, too, there was a heavy stink of crude oil afire in a burner below them. Dryway came clambering up, swearing because he had got filthed up.

Humble said, 'Shut up, Tom. If we get away with this it is worth a few ruined suits.'

Dryway got to work again on the tackle and succeeded in hoisting the lid. Then the sullen convicts were driven to the task of lifting up the carboys and emptying the acid sludge into the sulphonator.

When that was done and the fumes

were rising as the heat got through the metal skin of the pressure pot, Humble rapped. 'Now sling Old Mouthy in, and the can after him.'

Bronya knew what was in that sack, knew also the contents of that can. And she knew their importance not only to these men, Dryway and Humble, but also to many other Warren Bridge people — and to the Law as represented by the police and the F.B.I. outside.

She was in a panic, watching the convicts cross reluctantly to seize hold of that sack. Then she saw a distant movement down among the pots, and desperately she played for time. She called, 'I think I ought to tell you. I wasn't lost — I came here with three carloads of Feds.'

That stopped them, every one. They turned, and she saw she had their attention. She played boldly, sensing rather than seeing that approaching figure.

'There's an army of them camped outside. You'll not get away with this.'

Dryway rapped. 'The blazes with her.

Get these parcels in and then we can talk to her.'

Out of the corner of her eye she saw someone stand upright, and there was the gleam of light on a gun barrel. Gladness overwhelmed her.

For exactly five seconds.

Then a voice came through that was thin and dry as the crackling of nutshells. It said, 'Looks like I came in time. Get your hands high, the lot of you.'

Bronya saw a smallish man, a man of such indeterminate age that he could have been anything from twenty to forty. He was wearing ill-fitting clothes and heavy boots, like those on Egghead's and Delcros's feet.

She heard Johnny Delcros gasp, 'Joe Guestler! What — '

And his hands clawed very high, very quickly. Egghead stood in a crouch, ready to spring, his face drawn in white fury. He said, 'How the hell did you get here?' and Guestler was so cocky he told them.

'You shoved old Rocky Whitwam and his mate into that laundry bin, back at the jail, didn't you? They found me there, unconscious. When you'd gone they got me out. I told Rocky I'd started to come after you and got knocked out coming down the chute, and he told me you were coming to see his brother to collect a million. That was a double-cross. I told Louie Savannah, and he had to decide on a jailbreak that day so's to get his hands on that dough. Only he went and broke his ankle.'

Johnny said, looking down the shed, 'Where's Jud Corbeta? He got away with you, didn't he?'

Guestler nodded. 'He's down in the yard, keeping watch.'

Plump Geordie Humble asked, 'You seen any G-men around?' He was anxious.

Guestler looked contemptuous. 'Not a smell of one. I guess the dame's tryin' to frighten you.' Then he went on to tell them how he had tracked them — and why.

'We got there in time to hear all that talk by those fellars back in Rocky's brother's house. And we didn't get much line on a million, so when thirty grand was mentioned we thought that would do nicely for us. We slept in a car in a garage at the Whitwam place, then came out here in another car we picked up yesterday. Looks like we got here in time.'

'In time for what?' demanded the belligerent Humble.

Guestler said, smiling coldly, 'Think, brother. In time to collect thirty grand.'

Humble shouted, 'The hell, you're not going to find any thirty grand. I took good care to hide it when I got outa the car.'

Guestler looked across at Egghead and Johnny. 'Looks like I need your help,' he said, and there was regret in his voice. 'This is one thing I can't do and watch you all the time. You're a coupla dirty, double-crossin' chisellers, but I'm big an' I'll forget it.'

Egghead and Johnny were already beginning to understand and were lowering their hands. Guestler said, 'We split four ways, huh?'

Egghead and Johnny nodded, faces relaxing into tight smiles, Johnny said, heartily, 'Sure we'll split four ways, Joe.'

But nobody looked at each other. For everyone was thinking: that four into thirty grand didn't go too well, and maybe there'd be a few less at the share-out. Egghead took the gun from Humble.

Joe Guestler said, 'This guy came prepared to pay up thirty grand. I guess it's stashed somewhere around, but we ain't got time to pull this joint to pieces. Instead, let's pull this guy to pieces until he talks. *Hang him inside that acid bath!*'

Dryway started to come forward, but that gun swung and sent him cowering back along with the shaken Bronya. Egghead and Johnny walked towards the plump Geordie Humble. He had guts. In desperation he lashed out.

Johnny Delcros slipped under the blow and started to belt him about the face. When he'd got the bewildered chemical manufacturer staggering, he and Egghead grabbed him and slung him into the acid bath.

He started screaming. It was too much for Bronya and she started screaming, too. Anyway she thought it was one way of trying to bring help.

It wasn't enough for Egghead, to have Humble hanging there with his legs in the acid. He started slapping him across the face and shouting, 'You two-timing — ! Where've you hidden that dough? Come on, talk!'

Humble changed his mind about not speaking and opened his mouth to say where the money was hidden.

Then something big dropped on top of Bronya and flattened her to the stage flooring. Simultaneously several guns roared.

Bronya saw Egghead reel and the movement knocked Humble into the big metal pressure pot, and they heard him scream until his head went under the acid inside. Twice after that they heard him scream, and then he was silent.

But no one could go and help him.

Bronya found herself rolling inside the arms of someone. She knew it would be Lief Sorensen, without seeing his face. It was painful, going under that heavy weight on the unyielding metal flooring, but after her recent plight she wouldn't have minded if they'd rolled a hundred yards.

Then they were behind cover, and Sorensen rolled clear and got to his knees. Now she could see that the G-men had crept up close along the various gantries and were firing their automatics whenever they saw a target. Tom Dryway was crouching in a corner, white-faced, and hoping to hell he wouldn't stop a stray.

For the fight was between the three cornered convicts and the G-men now. They were behind the cover of a sulphonator, and they would take some shifting. That was, until Sorensen created a diversion.

He looked up, nodded, then dived head first across to the shelter of a nearby pressure pot, firing as he went through the air. Someone else dropped lightly down onto the gantry. It was Ben Arcota, Bronya saw. It was a long drop, but Ben was perfectly poised and upright when his feet hit the deck, and his gun was blazing nonstop. Sorensen came staggering painfully back at that — he had hurt his shoulder in that dive — and his gun gave out its last two rounds.

Egghead sat down and started coughing over a smashed chest. Johnny Delcros twisted to his feet, clawed at nothing, and then pitched over the iron railing on to the ground floor, twelve feet below. Joe Guestler said, cynically, 'Okay, I've had enough,' and dropped his gun.

*    *    *

Everyone walked very slowly across the waste lot towards the cars that were being driven up. After that acid-ridden atmosphere it felt good to be out in the sunshine again. Sorensen and his assistant were helping Bronya along, though after the first few strides she felt all right again and in fact said she thought they probably needed help and not she. So they all walked together in contentment. Bronya said, 'I see a good idea in ballet for G-men, Ben. The way you dropped over that railing . . . '

Sorensen said, with dignity, 'May I point out that I was first to make that drop?'

And Bronya said, 'May I point out that

you've been having to help me walk this last hundred yards in consequence? You're quite a weight, Mr. Sorensen.'

They laughed. It was very easy to laugh now, they found. So Sorensen said, with fairness, 'You don't know anything about ballet, Bronya. We were in a hell of a mess. We found we couldn't get in after you because a fellow took up guard just inside the yard. So Ben here said for me to throw him over that wall and he'd deal with the watcher. Which we did. You should have seen him as he flew through the air with the greatest of ease, and by the look of him he must have landed full weight on the unfortunate Jud Corbeta.'

They got into the car, while the police chief said, with heavy satisfaction, 'Now, that was a nice bit of work. I'm goin' to remember all that. All that's left is for a judge and jury to do a bit of tidying up — there's the Conscience of America, those danged old interfering idiots, the lynch mob and three escaped convicts. They'll get tidied up all right, I reckon.'

Then he saw that Sorensen and the girl weren't listening, so he complained, 'Am

I talkin' to myself? What are you two fixing?' suspiciously.

Sorensen held Bronya's hand and told him. 'I'm fixing for Ben to go back to the field office to report without delay.'

That straw head came round in wide-eyed surprise. 'The hell,' said Ben Arcota, and he was suspicious, too. 'Maybe you'll tell me why?'

Said Sorensen calmly, 'You don't think I want you around the place when I'm fixing to stay out at Bronya's over the weekend, do you? She says her father'll like me.' Butter wouldn't have melted in his mouth.

And her father did. But not as much as his daughter, of course.

## THE END

We do hope that you have enjoyed reading this large print book.

Did you know that all of our titles are available for purchase?

We publish a wide range of high quality large print books including:
**Romances, Mysteries, Classics**
**General Fiction**
**Non Fiction and Westerns**

Special interest titles available in large print are:
**The Little Oxford Dictionary**
**Music Book, Song Book**
**Hymn Book, Service Book**

Also available from us courtesy of Oxford University Press:
**Young Readers' Dictionary**
**(large print edition)**
**Young Readers' Thesaurus**
**(large print edition)**

For further information or a free brochure, please contact us at:
**Ulverscroft Large Print Books Ltd.,**
**The Green, Bradgate Road, Anstey,**
**Leicester, LE7 7FU, England.**
**Tel:** (00 44) **0116 236 4325**
**Fax:** (00 44) **0116 234 0205**